Other Series by Harper Lin

The Patisserie Mysteries

The Emma Wild Holiday Mysteries

The Wonder Cats Mysteries

www.HarperLin.com

Lattes, Ladyfingers, and Lies

A Cape Bay Café Mystery Book 4

Harper Lin

ISBN-13: 978-1987859348
ISBN-10: 1987859340

Contents

Chapter One

I hummed as I stacked boxes in the back room of the café. I couldn't have been in a better mood. I was due to fly to Italy with my boyfriend, Matt, in seven short days, and I was so excited I could barely contain myself. I picked a pack of napkins out of the shipping box, pirouetted to the shelves behind me, and made my best attempt to set the box on the shelf with the grace of a ballet dancer. It had been more years than I cared to think about since I'd last taken ballet, though, so I was pretty sure it looked more awkward than graceful.

I spun again and plucked another box from the shipping container. "La-da-da, da-da-da, da-da-da, da-da-da, la-da-da-daah!" I sang. "Da-da-dah."

"'*That's Amore*'?" Sammy asked from the doorway.

I jumped into the air—and not a graceful ballerina jump either. My hand flew to my chest as I turned to look at her. I could tell from the burning sensation that my cheeks flamed.

"What?" I was so startled I couldn't remember what she'd said, only that she'd caught me smack in the middle of my Dean Martin/Gene Kelly song-and-dance routine.

Sammy pressed her lips together and blinked hard, but she couldn't hide the twitching in her cheeks as she tried to keep from laughing. "You were singing 'That's Amore,'" she said as evenly as she could.

"Was I?"

"Mm-hmm." Her blue eyes twinkled.

I shrugged, trying to play it cool. "My grandmother used to play it a lot. It gets stuck in my head sometimes."

"I'm sure." She laughed. "It couldn't possibly have anything to do with a certain trip to a certain foreign country with a certain man."

If it was possible, my blush grew even deeper.

A laugh bubbled up out of Sammy's throat. "Don't worry, Fran. It's our little secret." She stepped into the room and grabbed the box I'd put on the shelf. "I just need some more napkins for the counter, and I'll be out of your way." She flashed me a smile and disappeared back into the café.

I waited for a few seconds with my eye on the doorway in case she came back then returned to unpacking. I found myself still humming but managed to keep my dancing mostly in check as I emptied the last few supplies from the box. When I was done, I broke down the box and tossed it out the back door with the recycling, perhaps with a bit more of a flourish than I normally would have.

As I walked back inside, I lingered in the doorway between the storeroom and the café, surveying the space with a slight smile on my face. It was simple and cozy, and no place in the world felt more like home to me. I had spent nearly as much time inside these walls as I had inside my own house. The exposed brick walls, the mismatched tables and chairs, the handwritten menu hanging high on the wall—they had all been the same for as long as I could remember, since I was a child running around and getting in the way as my grandparents and my mother served coffee, sandwiches, and desserts to the people of Cape Bay, Massachusetts. I considered it both a duty and a privilege to be the sole proprietor of Antonia's Italian Café, the business that had been my immigrant family's life work.

The café was moderately full, pretty much what I expected on a mid-October Tuesday afternoon. A group of women clustered in the armchairs in the corner, ostensibly for their book club meeting, but I hadn't seen any of them crack a book yet. They sat with their lattes and ladyfingers or scones or—for the daring few—cupcakes and chatted. Rhonda, who worked for me part time, was one of them. She caught my eye and waved. The Mommy Brigade, she called them—a group of mostly stay-at-home moms, who got together while their kids were in school to relax and enjoy one another's company.

A few other customers were at the café tables along the wall: a couple of retirees, some people on break from their jobs at other shops along Main Street, others just enjoying a cup of coffee and a few quiet moments to themselves.

Sammy bustled around behind the counter, checking to make sure we had plenty of clean dishes on the shelves, straightening things up, and exchanging a word here and there with the customers. I knew the name of almost everyone in the room, and I recognized the faces of most of the rest of them. The tourist season was all but over in our small beach town, but ironically, it was actually busier than it usually was on a weekday afternoon at the height of the season. It was as if all the locals hid in their homes when the vacationers were around and came out again when things were quieter.

It was busier but somehow easier to manage at the same time. The vacationers came in noisy packs that were confused, demanding, or both—multi-generation families who seemed to think we were a full-service restaurant, groups of college students who assumed we served cocktails, New Yorkers who thought we were Starbucks and couldn't be bothered to order in normal English. None of that from the locals—they came in, ordered something we actually sold, and sat down to enjoy their drinks without snapping their fingers or yelling at Sammy or me when they wanted sugar for the coffee they'd only moments before sworn they wanted black. The locals were more laid back—busy enjoying their everyday lives and the company of their friends, not trying to make the café and its offerings into something they weren't.

A man came in, and Sammy greeted him with her trademark brilliant grin. She moved to fill his order almost as soon as he started talking. She had a plate topped with a paper doily resting on the counter, ready for his dessert order before he had even finished paying. After handing him his card and receipt, she picked up the plate and stepped over to the case displaying our array of baked goods. She put a glove on one hand and slid the case's door open with the other. She reached her gloved hand into the case and pulled out a small handful of ladyfingers. Instead of putting them on the plate, she stopped and looked into the case. She stood up suddenly and turned toward me.

"Fran?" she said loudly then jumped when she saw me standing in the doorway. "Oh! I didn't realize you were right there!" She paused for a second, looking thrown off by me not being deep in the back room. We were getting good at this startling each other thing today. "Um." She hesitated. "Can you check on whether we have any more ladyfingers in the back? We're all out up here."

"Sure thing." I went back into the storeroom and checked the box of ladyfingers. Crumbs. Usually we were better than that at keeping track of our stock.

I picked up the phone to call Monica and ask her to bring some more when she delivered our next batch of tiramisu and if she could bring more than last time. Monica owned her namesake Italian restaurant in the next town. She served the most delectable desserts, including her homemade tiramisu. It was absolutely one of the best things I'd ever tasted, although, to be fair, just about everything *Osteria di Monica* served was incredible.

Back in the summer, we'd worked out a deal for me to sell her tiramisu in our café. Monica delivered it a few times a week, and it was by far our top-selling sweet. A few weeks ago, it had finally dawned on me that the ladyfingers she made for the tiramisu would be great for dipping in coffee. As soon as Monica's first batch landed in the display case, customers snapped them up faster even than I'd expected, as evidenced by our empty display case.

I spent a few minutes chatting with Monica on the phone after I let her know we'd need an extra batch. She was predictably unsurprised that they were selling so well. She never lacked in confidence when it came to her cooking and deservedly so. She wouldn't let me off the phone until we'd had a nice chat about my upcoming trip. She was almost as excited about the Italy trip as I was.

"I talked to Stefano," she said. "He and Adriana are looking forward to showing you Venice. I talked to them on the computer! It's remarkable what technology can do now. To think, I cannot just talk to my grandson half a world away, but I can see him too! We couldn't have dreamed of such things when I came here from Italy or even when Alberto was there, oh, twenty-five years ago now. And Adriana is lovely. I can't wait to meet her in person! I'm so looking forward to hearing what you think of her, Francesca."

Monica's grandson Stefano had been in Venice for nearly two years, learning proper Italian cooking so that he could come back and work in the family restaurant. Monica was more than a little excited that he was bringing his trained-chef girlfriend with him and not just because she could help out in the restaurant. Monica expected to hear news of a proposal any day.

In addition to Monica extracting a promise from Stefano to give Matt and me the grand tour, she'd also given me a list of all the places in the entire Veneto region where we needed to visit or eat. I was fairly certain we would barely have the time to visit a fraction of the places she'd told me about. We'd be there for two weeks, but our itinerary had us covering the entire country, from Venice and Verona in the north, down to Rome and Naples and even Sicily, so we wouldn't have much time to experience each place.

The bell over the door jingled, and a woman a few years older than me rushed in. She looked harried with her mousy-brown layer cut sticking out and her royal-blue sweater set pulled askew. She looked like a soccer mom who'd gotten a little too riled up about the wait in the carpool lane.

She gave a wave and said something to the book clubbers as she hurried past them on her way to the counter. She gave her order to Sammy and paid then darted back over to the circle of women in the corner, grabbing a chair and dragging it noisily over to their table. I noticed she did not have a book with her.

As Sammy prepared the drink, a couple of business types got up from their table and left. I wasn't sure of their names, but I recognized them as regulars. Sammy glanced in their direction and smiled.

"Thanks guys!" she called. "See you tomorrow!" I saw her eyes flit over to the table they had just left and the dishes scattered across it. We hadn't been working together long—only since I'd taken over the café after my mother's sudden death a few months ago—but I could read her mind.

"I'll get it." I walked over, piled the dishes up, and took them into the back, then grabbed a rag to take back to wipe down the table. I turned the bud vase on the table so the Peruvian lilies in it had their most attractive side facing out. The tin that held the sweeteners was a little low, so I grabbed a handful from the back and brought them out to disperse among the tables. I finished as Sammy got the disheveled woman's drink ready. "Here." I reached out for the cup and saucer.

"The woman in the blue." She nodded in the book club's direction. She hesitated when she realized three of the women in the group were wearing blue shirts.

"I saw her come in." I smiled.

"Thanks."

I took the cup and saucer in one hand and grabbed a handful of napkins in the other. The book clubbers always needed more napkins. Someone was always spilling her drink or pouring it on herself or needing to wipe her hands or her mouth or blot her lipstick. No matter how many napkins they had, they always seemed to need more. I sat the drink down in front of the disheveled woman in blue and put the napkins in the middle of the table.

"I thought you ladies might need some more of these."

"Oh, thank you!" one of them exclaimed, immediately picking one up and dabbing at an invisible spot on her blouse.

"Ellen always needs more napkins." Another nodded at Ellen, who was still studying her shirt to see if she'd gotten the spot out. Based on the two other women who had also immediately grabbed at the pile, I suspected Ellen wasn't the only one.

The woman who had spoken had her head tilted back at an awkward angle, and there was a band of light across the bottom of her face. I glanced at the window and saw that, indeed, sun poured in, trying to blind her.

"Do you want me to close these blinds for you?" I asked.

"Oh, please, yes! That would be wonderful."

"If you'll just excuse me one second..." I scooted behind one of the women as I wondered how the book clubbers all seemed to need things—napkins, the blinds closed—but didn't ask for any of them. It was especially odd since Rhonda sat right there with them. Surely they knew she worked at the café and would know that we didn't mind customers closing the blinds in lieu of squinting.

Certain the women needed something else—some sugar, a refill, directions to the restroom—I opened my mouth to ask if there was anything else I could do for them. Before I could say anything though, I realized why—today at least—they were all so reluctant to get up from the table.

Chapter Two

"Do they have any suspects?" Ellen asked, apparently satisfied that her blouse was clean.

Suspects? Suspects in what? I froze momentarily with my hand on the blind cord. Cape Bay had had an unsettling number of murders in the last few months, though otherwise, crime was very low. Sure, there was some petty crime, especially during the summer—teenagers "stealing" someone's beach umbrella by moving it five hundred feet down the beach, teenagers shoplifting bags of chips from the local convenience store, teenagers getting caught drinking—basically, a lot of teenagers getting up to no good. Other than that, Cape Bay was a safe place to live, the kind of place where people didn't lock their doors and kept their keys in their cars. Except for the murders. In the split second before the disheveled woman answered Ellen's question, I found myself hoping against hope that it wasn't another one of those and that some teenager had gone a little overboard and decorated the boardwalk with some spray paint.

"Not as far as I know. I mean, it's only been a few hours."

"I saw on TV that if they don't find a suspect in the first forty-eight hours, it's unlikely that they'll find one at all," the woman who'd had the sun in her eyes said.

"Well, it hasn't been forty-eight hours yet, has it, Diane?" Ellen snapped back at her. The two of them seemed to have some particular grudge against each other, the way they snipped at each other. I'd have to remember to ask Rhonda what their deal was.

Diane ignored her. "Who found her?"

My throat went dry as I hoped that the "her" in question was a car, not a woman. I made it a point to stay out of my customers' conversations unless invited, but in this case, I knew I had to butt in.

"Found her?" My voice came out all hoarse and scratchy.

Rhonda looked up at me and nodded slightly.

I closed my eyes and wished this wasn't happening.

"You hadn't heard?" Ellen asked.

Before I could shake my head no, Diane spoke up. "Well, none of us had before Susan came in and told us, did we?"

Ellen gave Diane a dirty look.

"Who was it?" I asked. The million-dollar question.

Everyone looked at the disheveled woman, who I now knew to be Susan.

"Georgina."

"Rockwell?"

Susan nodded.

I put my hand against the window frame to steady myself. Georgina Rockwell. She worked down the street at Howard Jewelers. I didn't know her well, but we'd chatted a few times, and the last time I'd seen her at the café, we'd talked about getting together sometime for drinks and to chat. That had been two days ago.

"What happened?"

Everyone looked at Susan again. She looked at her coffee and sighed. "There was a robbery at the jewelry store. Georgina got caught up in it somehow and—" She stopped and shook her head.

I stared at her in shock. I didn't know what to say. A robbery at one of our little Cape Bay shops was horrifying enough, but one that ended in murder? It sent chills down my spine.

"But what did they do to her?" Diane asked. "I mean, did they shoot her or...?" I couldn't quite blame her. I wanted to know too, but it seemed so... *crude* to ask. The other women seemed to feel the same way, based on the mix of horror and intrigue on their faces.

Susan shook her head. She leaned toward the rest of the women and dropped her voice down low enough so that anyone not at the table wouldn't be able to hear her. "They, um, used a brick to break the window. They threw it, and it hit her." She mimed something flying through the air and hitting her in the temple. I cringed at the thought.

"When?" I asked. "When did it happen?"

"Last night. Around ten, they said."

"Ten? Ten p.m.?" I couldn't believe I'd heard her right. Everything on Main Street closed by nine, especially at this time of year, when we hardly had a tourist outside of the weekends. In fact, I was pretty sure Howard Jewelers closed around five or six. I wasn't really sure, but I knew the shop was dark when I closed up the café each night.

Susan nodded.

"What was Georgina doing there at ten o'clock at night?"

She shrugged. "I can't imagine, unless they were doing inventory or something? But then Dean would have been there. I don't know."

"You never told us who found her." Apparently, Diane used that same snippy tone of voice with everyone, not just Ellen.

"Dean. The brick set off the alarm. The alarm company called Dean, and when he got there, there she was."

"Their alarm company doesn't call the police?" I asked. Ours did. Police first, me second.

"I guess not."

That seemed strange. The whole point of the alarm was to call the police. What was I going to do if the café was being broken into? Call the police, of course. For as much as I paid the alarm company every month, the least they could do was save me the trouble and call the authorities themselves. That way, the police would get there faster, and I'd be spared the trauma of finding the body of one of my employees. I looked over at Sammy and imagined responding to a late-night alarm call to find her bloody on the floor. I shuddered. It would be awful.

"Poor Dean," I said softly. Dean Howard was the Howard in Howard Jewelers. Well, his family was, anyway. The jewelry shop had been in his family for at least a couple of generations, selling engagement rings and Mother's Day gifts and First Communion necklaces to the men and women of Cape Bay.

Dean was several years older than me, so I didn't know him well when we were growing up, but I remembered both being intimidated by him and thinking he was impossibly cool when I'd try to go play on the playground at the park only to find him hanging out on the swings, always with a girl, and always puffing on a cigarette. Of course, that was back before it was quite so well known how bad smoking is for you, and in any case, the fact that he was breaking The Rules was probably what made him seem so cool in my childhood eyes anyway.

"Psshh," Diane interjected. "Dean's a hard-nose. It probably didn't even faze him."

"Finding one of his employees dead?" My voice came out a little louder than it should have. I glanced around the café with an embarrassed smile. Fortunately, the place had emptied out a little, so my outburst only served to disturb a few people. Sammy, though, gave me a concerned look from behind the counter. I tried to force a more natural smile but gave up and mouthed "I'll tell you later." She raised her eyebrows but went back to stacking dishes.

Diane shrugged. "Think what you want."

I gritted my teeth. Diane was the one who could think what she wanted. As far as I knew, she hadn't ever found a dead body. I had. It was one of the worst moments of my life. And that death hadn't even been bloody. I'd thought he was asleep… until I realized he wasn't. Diane could go fly a kite, as my grandmother would have said.

"He may still be down at the store," Susan said. "I think he had quite a bit of cleaning up to do."

I winced. I didn't want to think about the cleanup Dean would have to do. "Did you talk to him?" I was curious how she had so much information when I hadn't even heard about the break-in or Georgina's death.

"Oh, no!" She pulled her head back like the idea was revolting. "My friend Margaret works down at the police station. We had lunch together, and she told me all about it."

"Margaret Robbins?"

Susan nodded. Of course it was Margaret Robbins. She worked the front desk at the police department and was a known chatterbox. We'd gone to high school together, and she'd been the same way back then. If anyone would know all the details and freely share them, it would be her.

I leaned against the window and tried to process everything I'd heard. It was horrible. I admit I forgot I was intruding on my customers' space and conversation.

The jingle of the bell over the door brought me back to my senses. A group of five walked in, dressed in business clothes and carrying laptop bags and notepads. A couple of them glanced around, first at the big table where the book clubbers were gathered, then at the opposite side of the café that only had little two-tops. They made a beeline for the two-tops. Not that I could blame them. I'd had more than one coffee shop meeting when I was working in New York, and we always sat as far away from other people as we could. It was the only way we could actually manage to get anything done without being interrupted by nosy people eavesdropping and asking questions about what we were working on or hipster types who would immediately start going on loudly about how they could never sell out and go to work for The Man like us corporate drones, which was why they worked part time for minimum wage at a big chain bookstore. I couldn't imagine how distracting it would be to sit next to people discussing a murder.

Sammy caught my eye. I nodded and flashed her a smile. I knew she could handle a group that size with no problem, but why should she when I was there? I looked back at the book club women and smiled politely. "Is there anything else I can get you ladies?"

A couple of them shook their heads, and a couple glanced at the others before declining.

"No, we're fine," Diane said without looking at anyone else. I saw Ellen roll her eyes and Rhonda quickly look out the window.

"All right. Well, if I can get you anything, please let me know!" I paused as I walked past Susan's chair. "I apologize for interrupting. But thank you for sharing the information about Georgina." Susan gave me a weak smile and nodded. Out of the corner of my eye, I saw Diane make a face. What on earth was with that woman? I did my best to keep my expression neutral and joined Sammy behind the counter.

The business crew had pushed several of the two-tops together, dropped off their bags, and lined up at the counter. Sammy took the orders as I started filling them. Two black coffees, one hot tea, one iced tea, and one latte, ordered with a smile and a nod in my direction.

Lattes were my specialty. The method of preparation was something that had been perfected in my family over generations. My mother had started creating images in the lattes she made back in the late 1980s when latte art first became a thing, but she never really branched out beyond hearts and rosettes.

During the long hours I used to spend at the café after school when I was a teenager, though, I learned hearts and rosettes, then suns and moons and stars, rabbits, bears, flowers, scorpions, snowflakes, random patterns, and whatever else I could think of. My friends came in and started asking for more complicated designs—a beach scene, a mountain—and before long, everyone in town knew that little Franny Amaro could create some pretty amazing things in a latte. Whenever I came home from college for a break, I'd be put back to work in the café, and the locals would flock in to see what new designs I'd come up with.

Even though I'd been away for years after graduation, it hadn't taken long after I'd gotten back to work full time at the café for people to start coming in just to get me to make them lattes. Some of them, like the business guy who'd just ordered, I didn't even recognize, but somehow, they knew me. It was like being a kind of celebrity. Lattes were a weird thing to be known for, but I figured it was better than some of the things people were small-town famous for—the head cheerleader from twenty-five years ago, the teacher who married a former student, the guy who wrecked his father's brand-new lobster boat when he took it out drunk on prom night. I knew all of those people and had had more than one conversation that identified them that way.

"Who?" I'd ask when Sammy would refer to someone like I was supposed to know.

"Dave Sampson," she'd repeat. "You know, the one who got drunk and wrecked his dad's new fishing boat on prom night?"

"Oh, yeah!" I'd reply, suddenly clearly remembering Dave and the boat with the giant hole in the hull and the looks on his parents' faces as they took custody of him from the Coast Guard. Even though Dave was now a married father of four with a successful law practice in Boston, to the citizens of Cape Bay, he would always be known for the boat wreck. Compared to that, I was quite happy to be known for my milk-pouring skills.

I prepared each of the basic drinks—the black coffees and the teas—and set them on a tray as Sammy pulled the food—one cupcake, one tiramisu to share, and one mozzarella-tomato-basil sandwich—they'd ordered out of the display case. The man who'd ordered the latte lingered near the register when I started pulling his espresso shot. That wasn't really unusual. Plenty of people were as interested in the process of creating latte art as they were by the end product.

"Anything in particular you'd like?" I asked as I steamed the milk.

He shrugged and smiled. "Whatever you feel like making."

I nodded. I loved having creative freedom, but it was always a little anxiety inducing when the person knew my work but I didn't know them. I wanted to make something impressive, but I didn't know what would impress them. Some people were astounded by a well-done circle. Others weren't fazed unless it was competition worthy. I had no idea where on the spectrum this guy would fall, but the milk was ready, and I needed to pour. I tipped the pitcher over the cup. Two circles, one a little larger than the other. I grabbed a toothpick. Carefully, I used it to etch a ring around the bigger circle then added a series of pinpricks scattered around the cup.

He leaned across the counter. "Saturn!" he said, noticing the orb and rings. "And that's what? Uranus? And then the stars! That's amazing! You're as good as I heard!"

"Thank you." I blushed a little. I put the cup and saucer on the tray that Sammy was waiting to take over to the tables the group had pushed together. The guy lingered for an extra couple of seconds and smiled at me before walking over to the table. I wiped down the espresso machine. Sammy dropped the drinks and food off at the table and came back around the corner.

"So..." She leaned against the counter and nodded at the book clubbers, who were starting to get up. "What was that all about?"

"Let's go in the back room."

Chapter Three

Sammy covered her mouth with her hands. Tears filled her eyes. "Oh, my God. Georgina?"

I reached out and rubbed her shoulder.

"I can't believe it. She was here yesterday. She sat right there at the table in the corner. She had a latte and ladyfingers. I told her how pretty her hair was." She sniffed and looked at me. Mascara pooled under her eyes. "She'd just gotten it done. It was a really pretty red—suited her really well."

I pictured Georgina in my mind. Red really would suit her. Her naturally brown hair had red undertones to begin with, and punching them up would have really brought out her coloring. I imagined her thick waves framing her face in a curtain of red. She'd been pretty to begin with, but I had a feeling she'd have been a stunning redhead.

Just thinking about how she would never style her hair again, never get to take advantage of her new color, made me sad. For some reason, it was always the stupid, little stuff that hit me the hardest when someone died: a new haircut that wouldn't be enjoyed, a bag of souvenirs that would never be given to the family members eagerly awaiting them, the just-purchased bottle of perfume my mother never got to wear. Out of all the tragedies of a sudden death, those things most tore me up inside.

I grabbed Sammy and hugged her. She clung to me, burying her face in my shoulder. At least my shirt was black so the mascara stain wouldn't show. We stood like that until we heard a tap on the storage room door. I turned around to see Rhonda leaning against the doorframe.

"Looks like you've got another murder to solve," she said.

"I'm staying out of this one," I replied. "I think the police will appreciate it."

I'd managed to get myself involved in the investigations of three murders in Cape Bay since I'd come back to town over the summer. It wasn't that I thought of myself as an amateur private investigator or anything like that, just that I somehow kept getting drawn into them. I'd ask one innocent question, and—boom!—I was sucked in. My curiosity wouldn't let me let it go. I'd found some critical evidence in each case, but that didn't mean either the police—or I—were eager for me to go doing it again.

"Ryan said you were really helpful last time though!" Sammy said.

Okay, so maybe the police didn't mind my meddling so much. Ryan Leary was the newest addition to the Cape Bay Police Department, coming on right before the last murder we'd had back at the end of the summer. While he and Sammy would both deny there was anything going on between them, they sure seemed to spend a lot of time together.

"I'm leaving for Italy in a week. I have plenty to worry about besides solving Georgina's murder." I ticked off on my fingers. "What I'm going to wear over there, finalizing our itinerary, what I'm going to wear, making sure everything here at the café is in order, what I'm going to wear, making sure the dog is taken care of, what I'm going to wear."

Rhonda and Sammy both laughed, Sammy through her tears.

"You seem a little worried about what you're going to wear in Italy," Rhonda said.

"Italian women are very fashionable."

"Fran, you're Italian, and you're very fashionable. You're going to look fine. Better than fine. You're going to look great!" Sammy said.

I glanced down at my outfit: black top, black pants, black shoes—simple and boring. Fine for Cape Bay or even New York City, but I wasn't so sure about Italy. At least the shoes were Italian leather. My mother and grandmother had always emphasized to me the importance of Italian leather. "Nothing beats the quality," they'd told me, over and over again. Sure enough, I'd found that as long as I made sure the styles I purchased were classics, the Italian leather bags and shoes I purchased lasted forever. The shoes I had on were from college. Still, I wanted to blend in with the native Italians.

"I just don't want to stick out as an American."

"What's wrong with looking like an American?" Sammy asked.

"She means she doesn't want Matt's eye wandering to some gorgeous young Sofia Loren look-alike." Rhonda gave me a sly look. My cheeks turned pink.

"Matt wouldn't do that! You've seen the way he looks at Fran. He only has eyes for her!" Sammy said.

Even without a mirror to look in, I knew my face was bright red. I saw Rhonda try not to laugh, and I knew she'd noticed my flushed cheeks. I was afraid of what she would say next, probably something to send me flying out the back door, too embarrassed to show my face in the café ever again.

"I could take you up to Neiman's if you want. Little shopping trip. Just the girls," she said instead.

"I can cover the café for you," Sammy offered.

"Oh, no, you're coming with us, Sammy." Rhonda winked.

"Who's watching the café then? I can't leave Becky and Amanda here by themselves!" Becky and Amanda were the high school girls who worked at the café part time after school and on weekends. They were good employees, but I couldn't quite imagine the two of them running the café on their own, even for a few hours.

"They can come too," Rhonda said. "Team-building exercise. It won't hurt to close the café for an afternoon."

"They have school."

"We could go after school."

"It would be kind of fun," Sammy said.

I rolled my eyes. "I can't afford anything worth buying at Neiman's."

"You should get a part-time job," Rhonda said. "That's how I afford to shop there." Her part-time job, of course, was working for me at the café. She didn't make enough to afford anything substantial at Neiman Marcus either. She laughed. "I'm kidding... unless you want a key chain or some sticky notes, but those probably won't help you feel very stylish."

"They sell sticky notes at Neiman's?" I asked, completely thrown off by this revelation.

"Designer ones." She shrugged. "Or we could just go to Macy's."

"Oh, we should! It would be really fun!" Excitement shone from Sammy's face for a second before she sobered. "It feels wrong being happy when Georgina just died."

I nodded in agreement. It was a strange thing when someone you knew, but weren't close to, died. You were sad, but it wasn't the all-consuming kind of sadness that you had when a loved one died. Instead, you cycled through feeling sad, then feeling completely normal, then feeling guilty for feeling normal, then feeling sad again. I guess it wasn't all that different from when a loved one died, just less intense.

We stood, a little bit uncomfortable, thinking about Georgina and her heart-breaking death until the jingle of the bell over the café door jolted us out of our reverie. Rhonda turned to see who it was.

"Just Ryan." She glanced purposefully at Sammy. A look of excitement crossed Sammy's face, but she quickly regained her composure.

We listened to Ryan's heavy footfalls. Between his heavy cop shoes and his duty belt laden with his various cop accessories, his walk when he was in uniform was much louder than it was when he wore civilian clothes. I'd once asked him how on earth he managed to sneak up on criminals when he was always stomping around like that. He'd just smiled and said he had skills. I had to trust him on that.

His steps grew louder until he appeared in the storage room doorway. Rhonda scooted aside to give him space. That belt really did make him wide. He looked around at each of our faces, pausing a second on Sammy's. I stole a glance at her and saw her pretty blue eyes twinkle briefly. When he finished scanning the room, he crossed his arms across his chest.

"Well," he said, looking at me, "from the looks on all your faces, I'm going to say you already know Fran here has another murder to solve."

"What?" I shrieked. "Me? You're the one with the gun and the badge!"

"Hasn't stopped you before, has it?"

"Yeah, well, I don't think Mike would appreciate it very much if I went poking my nose around again." Mike Stanton was the head detective for the Cape Bay Police Department and a former high school classmate of mine. For the most part, he'd been tolerant of my amateur detective work, but I knew he'd prefer if I stayed out of things.

Ryan gave me a sly grin. "Considering you've solved his last three major cases, I don't think he'd mind too much."

"I didn't *solve* the last three cases."

"You didn't *not* solve them either."

I rolled my eyes. "Yeah, well, I'm leaving for Italy in a week. I don't need to get involved."

"Suit yourself." He shrugged.

"So it was a robbery?" Sammy asked after a few seconds.

"Looks that way." Ryan leaned his broad shoulders up against the doorframe. "Vic had no injuries except the blow to the head. You guys knew about that, right?" He'd been in town long enough to know how the gossip train worked around here.

"Yes, we did," I said. "And the 'vic' was named Georgina. She was a friend of ours."

"Right, of course, sorry." Ryan looked embarrassed. He was a good guy, but he occasionally forgot he was talking to civilians, not his fellow law enforcement officers. We didn't deal with crime and death in our everyday lives. At least, we hoped not to.

He straightened. "Georgina had no other injuries except the one to her head. It was a brick that hit her." He paused and looked around at each of us, seemingly to gauge whether this was new information. Deciding it wasn't, he went on. "We don't think whoever it was even expected her to be there. It was late, long after the store had closed, and all the lights were off. The medical examiner said that, based on the way she fell, she was crouched down behind the counter when the brick hit her. She would have been completely in the shadows. No way the perp could have seen her." He glanced at me as soon as the word perp passed his lips, as though to make sure I didn't object to it the way I had vic. The perp hopefully wasn't a friend of mine, though, and if by chance I did know the perp, I wasn't particularly eager to hear his or her name in connection with Georgina's murder, so it didn't bother me.

A horrible thought crossed my mind. "She was crouched down behind the counter? She didn't—did she—?" I struggled to put my thought into words, not wanting to say it out loud in case that somehow made it true.

Ryan caught on to what I was afraid to ask. He shook his head. "We watched the security footage. Dean has that place wired up. I mean, it makes sense with all the jewelry in there, but man, that's a lot of cameras. Anyway, we watched it, and Georgina didn't show any signs of seeing or hearing anything out of the ordinary. She walked out of the back room and over to the counter, totally calm. Never saw it coming."

That made it better, I supposed. At least she hadn't been afraid.

"Did they take anything? If you're calling it a robbery, they must have taken something, right?" Rhonda asked.

"One ring."

"One ring? A whole store full of jewelry and they stole one ring? They murdered Georgina, and all they stole was one ring?" She sounded offended at the thought.

"It was the most expensive thing in the store."

Rhonda scoffed and rolled her eyes.

"Do you think they even knew they killed her?" I asked.

Ryan hesitated and made a face. I wasn't sure he wanted to tell us. Slowly, he seemed to make up his mind. "They knew." I could practically see the cop part of his brain fighting with the normal part as he debated exactly how much to say and how to say it. "Based on where she fell, they would have had to step over her on their way in and out. And they used the brick they threw through the window to smash open the case. Plus, there was a lot of–" He hesitated, apparently seeing the horrified looks on our faces. "–evidence on the floor. They, uh, couldn't have missed it."

The four of us looked at our shoes, the walls, the floor, anywhere but at each other, as we each tried to process–or not–what Ryan had just said. Our silence was broken by Sammy's sob. I looked over at her. She had her hands covering her face, and her shoulders shook. I moved to wrap my arms around her, but Ryan moved faster. He held her as she cried into his shoulder. The thought crossed my mind that it was a good thing his uniform shirt was black, or he'd have some nasty mascara stains to deal with and then immediately felt guilty for thinking about something so shallow and frivolous when Georgina was dead.

I caught Rhonda's eye, and she tipped her head toward the door. I followed her lead, and we both walked out into the café to give Sammy some time to regain her composure. I kicked the doorstop on my way out so she wouldn't feel self-conscious about people hearing her cry.

"Wow," Rhonda said as we both stood behind the counter.

"Yeah." I scanned the café for anyone who needed help or any tables that needed bussing, anything to keep me busy so that I wasn't just standing there, thinking about Georgina. At least if I was doing something, I could pretend she wasn't front and center in my mind. I knew, though, that I wasn't going to be able to stop thinking about her until her killer was found. I was so chilled by the coldheartedness of someone just stepping over her like that and leaving her there to die.

"So are you still planning to stay out of it?" Rhonda studied my face like she was trying to find some clue to my intentions.

I was torn. I was sickened by Georgina's death, but I wasn't a police officer or a private detective. I was a normal, average, everyday citizen who was leaving on the vacation of a lifetime in a few days. I knew what I had to do. "Yes. I'm going to stay out of it."

Chapter Four

Later that night, I was alone as I got ready to lock up the café for the night. Sammy had left earlier in the afternoon, shortly after we found out about Georgina. She was understandably upset, and she'd opened that morning, so I sent her home. Ryan politely offered to escort her. Rhonda and I exchanged mischievous glances but didn't say a word.

Rhonda wasn't scheduled to work that day, but Amanda had called in sick, so Rhonda stayed and helped me out until she had to leave so she could get dinner ready for her husband and two boys. I didn't mind working alone. There was the usual after-work surge of customers, and then things died down. I waited until the last person left and started cleaning, even though it wasn't quite closing time yet. Matt was making me dinner, and I was looking forward to a long, quiet evening with him and Latte, my sweet little Berger Picard dog.

Once the place was clean to my perfectionist standards and everything was ready to go so Sammy wouldn't have to scramble in the morning, I set the alarm and left out the front door, locking it behind me. Briefly, I stared at the large plate-glass windows covering the front of the café. I'd never thought before about how easy they must be to break. It was a little scary to think about. At least we didn't have hundreds of thousands of dollars of jewelry sitting around. And more importantly, none of my employees were inside. I don't know what I'd do if something happened to one of them in my café. I'd be devastated. *Poor Dean.*

I glanced down the street and saw Howard Jewelers all lit up. Every light must have been on—every light except the Howard Jewelers sign over the door. That was out, a subtle-but-clear sign that the store was closed. I thought about going by to see if Dean was there and if he needed anything, but I knew Matt probably had dinner almost ready, and I didn't want to keep him waiting.

My cell phone rang in my jacket pocket. I pulled it out and looked at the caller ID. *Matty.*

"Hello!" I sang into the phone.

"Hey, Franny. You still at the café?"

I cringed. He probably had everything ready, the table all set, the wine glasses poured, and I was still at work. I hurried down the sidewalk toward home. At least it wasn't a long walk. "I'm just leaving."

"Oh, good."

Maybe he didn't have dinner ready after all.

"I had a meeting that ran late, and then I had to finish up some stuff. I'm getting packed up. I'm really sorry. I'll be home in about half an hour."

"Do you want me to pick something up for dinner? You can cook another night?"

"No, no, I'll do it. It won't take me long." I could hear him breathing heavier as he walked out to his car.

"Okay, if you're sure."

"I'm sure."

I suspected he was so adamant about it in part because he didn't want me paying for takeout. It was a long-running battle between us: who would pay for dinner. Matt had gotten pretty devious—handing his card to the hostess on the way in, calling ahead at our favorite places and giving them his card number. Once, I'd even caught him slipping the waiter a fifty when he handed back his menu at the beginning of the meal. I managed to pay that time, but Matt was winning overall, partly because, working in another town, he could pick up dinner on the way home and surprise me with it.

"Okay, so, I'll see you in a little bit then. Drive safe."

"Walk safe."

There was a pause for a few seconds. We hadn't yet said, "I love you," even though I was ready, and I suspected he was too. As a result, lately, every time we got off the phone, there was an awkward pause where we each wanted to say it but couldn't quite do so.

"Um, bye then."

"Bye."

I disconnected the call and slid my phone back into my pocket. I looked back down toward Howard Jewelers. The lights were still on. If Matt wasn't going to make it home for half an hour and still had to make dinner, I should have plenty of time to go check on Dean. My mind made up, I headed for the jewelry store.

I stopped outside the store and surveyed the interior. Normally stocked full of pretty, sparkly bracelets, necklaces, and rings, the cases were empty. From where I stood, I saw that the case in the back corner, farthest from the door, the one where Dean kept all the most expensive baubles, had a gaping, roughly brick-shaped hole in the top.

At the opposite corner of the store, one of the windows facing the side street was boarded over with plywood. Beneath it, a blue tarp was spread out across the floor. I looked away quickly and hurried around to the back of the store. An SUV I thought was Dean's was parked in one of the three spots. I pushed the buzzer next to the back door and looked up toward the camera with the glowing red light above it. If I were Dean, I'd certainly be cautious of people trying to get into the store through anything but the front door.

After a couple of minutes, I heard the locks click, and the door opened. Dean looked tired and older than he had the last time I'd seen him the week before. "Hey, Fran." He leaned against the doorframe and propped the door open with one hand.

"Hi, Dean." I waited a few seconds to see if he would invite me in. "Can I come in?" I asked when he didn't.

"You planning to steal anything?"

"Nope."

"Come on in then." He pushed off the doorframe and held the door open for me.

The storeroom was stacked with bins and boxes I suspected weren't usually there. They covered the shelves, the table, and most of the floor. The couch was wedged into the space under the stairs leading to the apartment on the second floor.

"I'd offer you a chair, but..." Dean's voice trailed off as he waved at the disaster that had taken over the room.

"That's okay. I don't plan to stay long... unless you want me to, of course."

"No, I'm about done here." He sighed heavily and ran his hand through his hair.

"How are you doing?"

He shook his head the slightest bit. "I've had enough here to keep my mind off things today. Tomorrow—I don't know."

I nodded sympathetically.

"It's my fault."

"What?" Had Dean done something to cause Georgina's death?

"I feel like it is, anyway."

"Why? What did you do?"

"I left her here alone. I left that ring out in the case instead of locked up in the safe. I could have had bars on the windows. I just never thought we needed them. In all the years we've been here, we've never had them. They seemed like something you'd see in the big city, not in Cape Bay. Stuff like this doesn't happen here."

"You're right. Stuff like this doesn't happen here. That's why you can't blame yourself. You never could have seen this coming."

"That's no excuse. I should have been more prepared." He rubbed his face with his hands. "I feel so guilty."

"It wasn't your fault," I repeated, hoping that hearing it enough times would make him believe it.

He rubbed his face up and down a few more times then ran his hands across his hair. "That damn ring. It's been more trouble than it's worth since the day I bought it. And trust me, it's worth a lot. A lot."

"How much?" I asked, even though I knew I probably shouldn't.

"Fifty."

Fifty. It took me a second to realize what he meant, and when I did, I almost choked. "Fifty thousand?" I could buy a car with that. I could buy two cars with that.

"Yep. Most expensive thing I ever bought, and it's sat in that display case ever since. Once in a while, some bride-to-be comes in wanting to look at it, but it's still just sitting there. Lot of capital tied up in that thing."

"Was it insured?"

"Are you kidding? Of course it was insured! I may have been stupid for buying it, but I'm not that much of an idiot."

I thought for a second. There was something he'd said that I wanted to know more about. Then I remembered. "You said it was more trouble than it's worth. Because no one's bought it or something else?"

"It was everything. Let me tell you." He folded his arms across his chest. It was a little intimidating, but there was no reason he'd want to intimidate me. "First, I bought it at an estate auction. I actually got a pretty good deal on it, but right after the auction ends, one of the family members gets all up in arms because she claims she didn't know the ring was being sold. So I end up having to fork over some extra cash to make her happy. Funny how an extra thousand suddenly makes it not such an important family heirloom."

I couldn't really relate.

"This is back when my dad was alive. I bring it back. He barely glances at it, says it'll never sell. It's going to sit on the shelf. I shouldn't have wasted all of that money. All of his money. When I own the store, I can make the decisions. He wanted to put it up for auction again right away. Someplace fancy. Christie's, Sotheby's, something like that—it was that good. I said no. He put me in charge of buying. I bought this. We were keeping it. He never really forgave me for that. Every time money got tight, he'd bring up the ring. 'We oughta sell that thing, you know.' But that would prove him right, and I couldn't let him win. After he died, I thought about finally selling it at auction, but I couldn't do it. It's too noteworthy now. Everyone in the area knows I have it. If I just sold it at auction, people would start to think that I needed the cash or something— that the store wasn't doing well. They'd start to suspect that maybe our quality wasn't the best. They'd stop coming here and start going someplace up in Boston. Can't do it. Can't do it. Damn thing costs me more in insurance money every month than the entire rest of the store."

He finally stopped to take a breath. While I didn't quite know if his logic was totally sound, I sympathized with how strongly he felt about it. If I thought the survival of Antonia's depended on something, I would fight for it, even if it cost me a fortune.

"You think someone knew how valuable it was, and that's why they stole it? To sell on the black market?" I didn't even know if the jewelry black market was a thing, but it seemed like it probably was. "Or do you think someone wanted it and couldn't afford it?"

"Neither."

"Neither?"

"I think the robbery was a cover-up."

"A cover-up?"

"I think they came to kill Georgina."

I gasped. Sweet, kind Georgina? It was bad enough to think she was killed accidentally, but on purpose? Who would do that? And why?

Dean saw my reaction and nodded. "I think they came to kill Georgina, and the robbery was just a cover-up. I mean, think about it. Why would a robber take just one thing? Why wouldn't he take as much as he could?"

"Because the ring was all he wanted?"

"That's a sweet idea, Fran. Real romantic. But guys don't break into jewelry stores because they want something. They break in so they can fence the stuff and get the money."

"Fifty thousand isn't enough money?"

"You don't get full price on the black market, Fran. No, a real thief would have taken everything he could get his hands on. Smash and grab. Maybe aim for the ring, if he knows it's here, but take everything around it. But this guy didn't do that. This was no robbery."

"Why would someone kill Georgina?"

"Because he hates her. Or loves her and doesn't want anyone else to have her."

He said it with such intensity I took a step back.

"No, not me. Her ex-boyfriend, Alex. He couldn't get over her breaking up with him."

"Is he a violent guy?"

"He didn't beat her up or anything, but he was the jealous type. Couldn't stand her not being with him anymore."

"And you think he killed her."

"I do." Dean's eyes fixed on mine, almost like he was daring me to argue with him. I wasn't going to.

"Did you tell the police that?"

"Of course. They didn't believe me, though. Blinded by the price tag on that ring. They're going to be out looking for it in pawnshops and not even look into Georgina's life. I told you it was more trouble than it was worth."

I wondered about that. I knew Mike was thorough, and I was sure he would investigate every lead, but if they were already so sure it was a robbery, might they overlook Georgina's ex?

"Fran." Dean stepped closer to me. "You nosed around on the murders earlier this year. Do you think you could help me out on this? Help Georgina out?"

"I–" I was cut off by my phone ringing in my pocket. I pulled it out. *Matty.* "One second." I held a finger up to Dean. "Hi," I chirped into the phone.

"Hey, where are you?"

"Oh, I just stopped off to talk to someone on my way home. I'll be there in a few."

"Okay, I'm going to get dinner started then. I'll see you soon."

"Okay. See you soon."

The awkward pause.

"Bye," Matt said finally.

"Bye."

"So will you help me, Fran? Help Georgina?" Dean made that intense eye contact again.

I knew what I had to do. "Yes, I will. I will do it for Georgina." It was the truth. And I already had my first suspect.

Chapter Five

"Hey, gorgeous." Matt greeted me at the door with a glass of wine. I took it with gratitude. He had no idea how badly I needed it.

"Hi." I leaned into him for a kiss.

"What's wrong?" He cupped my head in his hand. He had an uncanny ability to sense when something was off with me.

I took a deep breath and let it out slowly. "Georgina Rockwell was murdered last night."

"What?"

I felt tears spring to my eyes. I didn't know where they were coming from. Since hearing the news, I'd been shocked, horrified, and unsettled, but until that moment, I hadn't felt like crying. Matt pulled me into a hug and held me while I sniffled and cried on his shoulder. After a few minutes, I managed to regain my composure. I took a deep breath and a long gulp from my wine glass.

"Feel better?" Matt's warm brown eyes had a gentle smile in them as he looked down into my blue ones.

"As much as can be expected. I still feel sick about Georgina, but I think I'm all cried out for the moment."

"Good. Because I've tasted the sauce and it doesn't need any more salt."

I laughed involuntarily.

"Come on. Dinner's on the table."

"Let me guess—spaghetti Bolognese?"

"How did you know?" Matt asked in mock surprise.

"Lucky guess." Not really. It was the only thing he knew how to make.

He took my hand and led me through the living room and into the kitchen. His house was a small Cape Cod style, the mirror image of mine two houses down. When you walked in the front door, you faced the stairs to the second floor. To one side was the master bedroom, and to the other was the living room. In the back were the eat-in kitchen, the utility room, and the bathroom that also connected back to the master bedroom.

In the center was a fireplace that, back in the colonial period, would have opened into all three main rooms, but in our houses only faced the living room. All the houses on our street were actually Cape Cods. When they were built just after the Second World War, sameness was in style. All that distinguished one house from the next was the color, the plants in the garden plots, and the fact that some of them didn't have a second floor.

True to his word, Matt had dinner on the table in the kitchen—still in the pots he'd cooked it in, but I didn't care. Nothing wrong with saving a few dishes. To make up for the rough presentation, he'd lit candles and placed them in the center of the table, nestled among the pot with the spaghetti, the bowl with the bagged salad, and the plate with the garlic bread. He'd made such an effort to set up a romantic meal that I felt a little bad for bringing the news about Georgina.

"Where's Latte?" I looked around. Latte was my dog, and we were at Matt's house, but Matt usually used his key to my house to let Latte out when he got home so the poor little guy didn't have to wait for me to get done at the café. I was pretty sure Latte loved Matt almost as much as he loved me.

"Oh!" Matt made a beeline for the back door and pulled it open. "Latte!" he called into the dark.

"You left him outside?"

"It hasn't been long." He stepped out onto the patio.

"It doesn't matter how long! You can't just leave him out there!"

"I didn't just leave him." He came back inside with Latte's leash in his hand and Latte trailing behind him. "I tied his leash to the grill."

"You tied his leash to the grill? Matt!" I knelt down to pet Latte, who was so excited to see me he was prancing around the kitchen. "Oh, my poor baby! Did Matty leave you all by yourself outside? My poor baby!" I gave him a hug and let him lick my face.

"He didn't want to come inside when we got over here from your place. I think he likes the feel of the wind in his fur. He tried to lie down out on the front steps, but I figured the patio would be a better option since..." He paused, looking uncomfortable. "Uh, since there was stuff I could tie him to."

"Matty!" I rolled my eyes. At least he'd been trying to do something nice for Latte. I couldn't be mad at him for that. "I guess we'll just have to get you a little fence or something. Won't we boy? Yes, we will! Yes, we will!" I ruffled Latte's ears as I talked to him. It was kind of embarrassing to baby talk the dog like that, but at least I knew Matt didn't care. I'd caught him talking to Latte a time or two.

"Are you ready to eat?" Matt asked after giving me a few more seconds to play with Latte. "It's getting cold."

"Oh, is somebody jealous?" I asked him in the same tone I'd just used with Latte. I stood up and ruffled the hair behind his ears to drive home the effect.

"Aarrgghh!" Matt shook his head back and forth to try to get my hands off him. "Don't use that tone. It's weird!" He pulled away but laughed as he did it.

"Oh, you like it," I said playfully and pulled him close to kiss him. He smiled and kissed me back. After a minute, I pulled away. "Dinner's getting cold," I reminded him.

"I don't care." He kissed me again.

I pushed him away with a laugh. "I'm hungry!"

"Well, all right." He walked around the table to the chair I usually sat in and pulled it out for me. I sat, and he scooted in the chair. He served both of us and sat down across from me. "So tell me what happened to Georgina."

I felt suddenly and powerfully nauseous. I put down my fork even though I'd just picked it up. "Can we talk about literally anything else? I'll tell you everything I know later, but can we just talk about something else while we eat? I want to not think about it for a while."

"Because it's all you're going to think about until her murder is solved?" His fork hovered over his plate. "Don't forget we leave for Italy in a week."

"I know! Aren't you excited?" I seized my opportunity to change the subject. I picked my fork back up and took my first bite of the spaghetti Matt had made. It was delicious as usual. It might have been the only thing he could cook, but he did it very well.

Matt looked at me for a second then smiled and shook his head. "Yes, I'm excited."

"I talked to Monica today. She said Stefano will be happy to show us around Venice. I think she's actually as excited about our trip as we are. Maybe more, actually. She's very excited."

Matt chuckled. "I'm surprised she hasn't given us a shopping list yet." He paused and looked at me as I smiled. "Has she?"

I laughed. "No, she hasn't. But I won't be surprised at all if she does."

"Remind me to bring an empty suitcase."

"Oh, you already need one for all the shopping I'm planning on doing." Where better to buy some nice new Italian leather shoes or handbags than in the country where they were made? Maybe I could even find a little boutique where I could get something completely unique.

Matt groaned. "Do you think I can find a football game to watch on TV over there while you're doing all that shopping?"

"I think you can watch football, but not the kind the Patriots play."

"Ugh, soccer."

I laughed and bit into a piece of garlic bread. I could tell from the taste that he'd made it the way my grandmother used to—thick, crusty slices of bread toasted and drizzled with olive oil then rubbed with a freshly sliced clove of garlic. It was basically bruschetta without the toppings. Toppings were beyond Matt's skill level.

We talked about our plans for the trip through the rest of dinner, going over the hotels and tickets we'd already booked, the tickets we still had to buy before we left, the ones we'd get after we got there, the restaurants we wanted to go to, the sights we wanted to see. It was basically the same conversation we'd had every day for the past month, but neither of us had gotten tired of it. There was always some new activity one of us had only thought of or heard about, some detail we wanted to go over again, or something we just wanted to talk about again. It was the trip of a lifetime, and there was nothing else either of us could think about—at least not until this afternoon when I'd heard about Georgina's murder. Now the two things competed for space in my brain.

"You all finished?" Matt asked. Our conversation had drifted into a lull, and I was poking at my spaghetti with my fork as I let my mind wander.

"Hmm?" I murmured, raising my eyes up to his. I hadn't realized how distracted I'd been by my thoughts. "Oh. Yeah." I piled my silverware on my plate and pushed my chair back.

"I'll clean up." Matt stood up.

"But you cooked."

He shrugged. "You've had a rough day. I'll take care of it. Go play with Latte or something."

At the sound of his name, Latte lifted his head from where it rested on his paws. He lay in his normal kitchen spot, in the corner between the back door and the bathroom. From there, he could supervise all of our comings and goings while he waited for us to finish whatever we were doing that didn't involve playing with him.

"Well, I can't say no now, can I?" I grabbed a worn tennis ball from Latte's basket. Knowing what was coming, he popped up on his feet and danced around my legs. "We'll be out back." I flipped on the back light and let Latte out into the yard. I didn't bother putting his leash on. As long as there was a ball involved, I knew he wasn't going to wander off. I felt a moment's trepidation as I stepped outside. The light on the back of the house lit a fairly large area, but beyond that was darkness—and somewhere out there, a murderer.

I did my best to shake off the feeling. By all accounts, Georgina's murder hadn't been random. Either the store had been the target, or she had. I had no jewelry for anyone to steal, and I couldn't think of a reason why anyone would want to kill me, so I had no reason to be afraid. Besides, I knew Latte needed the exercise.

Latte pranced at my feet and nudged the ball in my hand. I smiled at him, pumped my arm a couple of times to get him excited, and threw the ball as far as I could. Latte took off after it. A few seconds later, he was back. I held out my hand, and he dropped the drool-soaked ball into it. I cringed a little then flung the ball again. I held my wet hand in front of me for a few seconds then wiped it on my pants. I'd spilled cold coffee on them earlier in the day. They had to be dry-cleaned anyway. What was a little dog drool on top of that?

We played fetch for ten or fifteen minutes until I heard the door open behind me. Matt slid his arms around me and kissed the side of my head. "Having fun playing drool ball?"

"A soggy time as always."

Latte ran back again, and this time, Matt held his hand out for the ball. Latte happily dropped it in, and Matt threw it for him, a lot farther than I could have. And then they did it again and again and again. And again. They probably could have gone on half the night, but it wasn't long before the October chill got to me, and I shivered.

"You cold?"

"A little." I folded my arms over my chest and tucked my fingers under them to keep them warm.

"Last one, okay, Latte?"

"You don't have to go in just because I'm a little chilly," I said through teeth clenched to keep them from chattering.

Matt chuckled and shook his head but didn't say anything. He just threw the ball again, even harder this time than before. Latte brought it back and dropped it in

Matt's hand. Matt bent down to scratch behind Latte's ears and was rewarded with a big, sloppy dog kiss to the face. "All right, buddy, let's go inside." He smiled at me. "You too, gorgeous."

Any other time, I would have at least tried to come up with a smart remark to crack back at him for ordering me around like the dog, but it seemed like I was getting colder by the second, so I was all too happy to comply.

"Coffee?" Matt asked. "Warm you up?"

I shook my head. "I need to sleep tonight."

"I have decaf," he offered with a grin that gave away that he already knew how I'd respond.

"No."

"Cocoa?"

"Yeah, that'll be good."

"Go sit down, and I'll get it ready."

"You're going to spoil me taking care of me like this."

"You deserve a little spoiling."

I went to the living room and sat down on the couch. Latte immediately jumped up next to me, laying his front paws across my lap and nuzzling his head into me. I took the hint and petted him. Not happy with only one hand stroking his fur, he wiggled farther onto my lap and shoved his head under my other hand. I scratched his head with one hand and stroked the fur along his back with the other.

Finally happy, he relaxed into me. From the kitchen, I heard beeping as Matt punched the buttons on the microwave to heat the water for our hot chocolate. I chuckled to myself. I was such a coffee snob that the idea of heating water in the microwave for just about anything was borderline horrifying to me. It wasn't the first time Matt had made me cocoa in the microwave though, and I knew it tasted good. I still found myself objecting to it on principle.

After just over three minutes—one and a half for each cup—Matt came into the living room with a mug in each hand. He handed me one and sat down next to me on the couch. I held my cup gingerly, hoping to keep Latte from jostling me and spilling it all over the both of us.

"So," Matt said, "are you ready to tell me about Georgina?"

Chapter Six

I stared into my cocoa. All I could think about was how weird her death was, but I didn't really want to talk about it—not the details of it anyway. If I could just skip to the whodunit part, it would be a lot less depressing. So I went over it all as quickly as I could and tried not to think about the scene inside the jewelry store. Matt rested his hand on my leg in a show of support as I talked.

"And even though I know I should leave it alone, I said I would help because I couldn't bear thinking about the possibility of Georgina's death going unsolved even a second longer than necessary, especially not when I already have a suspect."

"You think it's that Alex guy? The ex-boyfriend?"

"No. I think it was Dean."

"Dean? Really?"

"Mm-hmm. I think he staged the robbery, Georgina caught him in the act, and he killed her to cover it up."

"What makes you think that?"

"He was so focused on that ring and how much trouble it had caused him. He had more to say about that than he did about Georgina. And the way he talked about how guilty he felt and how it was his fault. He really seemed as though he meant it, like his guilty conscience was overriding his judgment and making him say things he really shouldn't."

"Are you sure it wasn't just that he felt responsible? If something happened to one of your girls in the café, you'd never forgive yourself. They could get struck by lightning standing outside, and you'd probably go apologize to their parents and try to turn yourself in to the police just on the basis of feeling as though you should have antici-pated a thunderstorm when there wasn't a cloud in the sky."

He wasn't wrong, but Dean wasn't me. "You didn't hear him though, Matty. He sounded like he really felt guilty."

Matt looked at me skeptically. "Is that it? He felt bad about his employee being murdered in his store, and he was annoyed about an expensive ring that he could have sold at any time."

"But he couldn't sell it. It's been sitting in his store for years!"

"He couldn't sell it because he didn't want to. He could have taken it to an auction somewhere or probably even to a store in Boston or New York. He didn't have to keep that ring."

"He said it would be embarrassing to sell it at auction because his store was known for having it."

"Exactly. He wanted to keep it. It fed his ego."

"But that doesn't eliminate him as a suspect. It just explains why he felt like he had to stage a robbery to get rid of it."

Matt raised an eyebrow at me. I hoisted my still nearly full cup of cocoa in the air as Latte scooted across my lap so he could sprawl across both Matt and me.

"For the insurance money."

"Yeah, I understood that." He raised his mug to his lips.

"Plus, he actually gets even more money out of it because he gets the fifty thousand from the insurance company–"

Matt choked and almost spit out his hot chocolate. "The how much?"

"Fifty thousand. Did I forget to mention that's how much the ring was worth?"

"Uh, yes. Yes, you did."

"Yeah. Fifty thousand."

"That's a lot of money."

"Now you see why I think he had a motive?"

"Yeah, I guess I do."

I gave him a "see, I told you so" look and picked up where I left of. "What I was saying is that he actually gets more money out of the ring by staging a robbery. He gets the *fifty thousand*"–I enunciated carefully–"from the insurance company, plus whatever he gets from fencing it."

"Fencing it?" Matt looked amused.

"Dean's word, not mine."

"It didn't sound like you." He chuckled.

I ignored him. "The other thing was how hard he was trying to convince me that it was Georgina's ex. He was absolutely certain that it was Alex. He didn't even admit the possibility that it could have simply been a robbery."

"Because it really was one."

"Exactly. And he told me all that right before he asked me to help him out by investigating, like he was trying to plant the idea in my mind."

Matt looked thoughtful and nodded.

"It smells fishy."

"Everything smells fishy, Franny. We live at the beach."

"It does not smell fishy! It smells beachy!"

"Same difference."

"Not really."

Matt shrugged and took a sip of his cocoa. I saw him look at me out of the corner of his eye. He was teasing me.

I rolled my eyes. "Besides, if he really thought the ex-boyfriend did it, why wouldn't he really push the police to follow up on that theory? I mean, he said he told them, but why would he tell them and then shrug his shoulders and ask me to investigate?"

"You are getting quite a reputation for your investigative skills."

I swatted at him. He ducked away, laughing, and barely avoiding spilling his cocoa. "The point is that I'm not buying it. He may have asked me to help, hoping I would buy the story about the ex and keep attention away from Dean, but all he did was convince me that he had means, motive, and opportunity." I ticked the three words I knew from cop shows off on my fingers.

Matt smiled at me, shook his head, then drained his cup. He set it on the end table next to him. Mine was almost gone too, so I finished it off and handed it to him. He put it next to his.

"How are you going to prove it?"

"Same as before. Talk to people. Ask questions. See what makes sense."

"As long as you stay safe and are finished by the time we leave next Tuesday, I don't care what you do."

"Well, according to a very opinionated woman at the café today, if they don't find a suspect in the first forty-eight hours, they're unlikely to find one at all."

"You already have a suspect. You just have to prove he did it. Did the very opinionated woman have anything to say about that?"

"Surprisingly, no. She had an opinion about pretty much everything else anyone said though." I told him quickly about Ellen and Diane and their incessant bickering. I was still curious about where the animosity between them came from.

"They sound fun," Matt said with more than a little sarcasm.

"Oh, they were."

"Well, as I said before, as long as you have it all wrapped up by next Tuesday, I don't care how long it takes you."

I laughed. "You don't care how long it takes, as long as it's less than a week?"

He smiled and pushed a stray strand of my long dark hair out of my face. "That's right."

"Oh, okay." I smiled back at him.

As Matt leaned in to kiss me, Latte hopped off our laps and headed for his water bowl in the kitchen.

* * *

The next day at the café, Rhonda hung out in the back with Sammy and me even though she wasn't scheduled to work. Her kids were at school, her husband was at work, her house was empty, and she was bored, so she came in to Antonia's. We weren't very busy, but she was pitching in with whatever she could, and of course, I was going to pay her for her time. I didn't have to, but it seemed wrong not to pay her. Besides, she was going to be picking up most of the slack at the coffee shop while I was in Italy.

When the café emptied out around mid-afternoon—no book clubs—the three of us gathered in the back room to talk. I leaned against the doorway as Sammy and Rhonda sat in the couple of chairs we had kept back there. Sammy, unable to keep her hands still, was fiddling with the papers on the desk. Rhonda and I clung to cups of coffee.

"I can't believe you're not going to at least ask a few questions about it," Rhonda said after a pause in our conversation about Georgina.

I hadn't exactly been moving around, but I froze completely, remembering that I'd told her the night before that I was going to stay completely out of the investigation into Georgina's death, only to change my mind a few hours later after talking to Dean.

"*Are* you going to ask questions?" She apparently noticed my hesitance and got excited about the possibility.

Sammy stopped fiddling with her receipts and looked expectantly up at me.

I sighed. "So I went and talked to Dean last night." I felt like I needed to explain myself. "And we talked for a while. By the end of it, I agreed to at least nose around a little bit. For Georgina. She doesn't deserve to have her murder go unsolved one second longer than necessary, and I feel I would be letting her down if I didn't at least try."

Sammy looked back down, but her hands remained still.

"Good," Rhonda said. "You'll figure it out. You have a knack for finding information other people don't."

"It's my years in PR. I learned how to get clients to tell me their dirty secrets so I could stay ahead of the rumor mill."

Before I moved back to Cape Bay from New York City, I'd worked in public relations for years. I was good at it, but it was tense and stressful. I never knew when the squeaky-clean celebrity I'd been peacefully representing for years was going to have a drug or sex scandal, or worse, when the clients I'd been working for tirelessly would lose their minds over an unflattering paparazzi picture, holding me personally responsible for its release, and telling my boss in no uncertain terms that I was incompetent and should be fired on the spot.

Compared to those, the clients who were always getting into trouble were a walk in the park. At least I expected drama with them, and even when the newspapers called with some new outlandish accusation, I wasn't really surprised and could reflexively answer, "no comment," without skipping a beat. Compared to that chaos, even the busiest days at Antonia's were exhausting, but not really all that stressful. At least the job had given me some pretty good investigative skills.

"Whatever it is, you're good at it. I know if I got murdered, I'd want you on the case," Rhonda said.

"Rhonda!" I exclaimed.

"Don't say that!" Sammy gasped.

"What?" Rhonda asked. "I didn't say 'when.' I said 'if.' The way things have been going around here the past few months, I wouldn't rule it out."

"Rhonda, don't say that!" Sweet Sammy was visibly disturbed by Rhonda's even suggesting that she might be the victim of foul play. I knew she was just being dramatic, and made a face somewhere between an eye roll and a scowl.

"Anyway, you've been on the case for what, twelve hours now? You have it figured out yet?" Rhonda asked.

"It's been more like eighteen."

"You probably have it solved then!" From anyone else, it would sound as if she was mocking me, but I knew she was looking for gossip. She wasn't much of one for sharing it beyond a small circle, but she loved to hear it.

"I wouldn't say that," I said.

"So what would you say?"

I shrugged. "Just that I have some thoughts."

"Thoughts you're going to share with us, right?"

I hesitated but only for a second. Sometimes, the best way to get information was to give some. "I have my suspicions about Dean."

"Dean? Really?" Rhonda leaned forward. "Why?"

"Something about his story didn't add up to me."

"Ooh, what?"

"It's hard to say. It's the way he was acting—like there was something he wasn't saying."

"They'd been fighting," Sammy said quietly.

"What?" I turned to look at her. Rhonda whirled around too. "Dean and Georgina?"

Sammy nodded.

"How do you know?"

"Georgina told me. When she was here. The day before she died."

"Did you tell Ryan?"

She nodded again. "He said they'd look into it."

"What were they fighting about?" Rhonda asked.

"She didn't say. All she said was that Dean was mad at her again. He chewed her out. She kind of laughed it off, said that's why she was down here—she needed a break from him."

I stared at her.

"Well, I guess you've got your motive, huh?" Rhonda turned back to me.

"I guess..." I let my voice trail off.

"What?"

"I don't know. I just—" I looked at her with my forehead wrinkled up. My grandmother would have told me to stop frowning before I gave myself wrinkles. "You know the ring that was stolen?"

Rhonda nodded. Sammy seemed to be lost in thought, although I suspected she was still paying attention.

"My theory was that Dean staged the robbery to get the insurance money, Georgina caught him in the act, and he killed her to protect himself. But what if..." I trailed off again, trying to find the words that felt the least awful to say out loud. Somehow, a spontaneous murder seemed less evil than a premeditated one.

"He killed her and staged the robbery to cover it up?" Sammy asked, proving that she really was paying attention.

I nodded. "Do you think he could have been that angry with her?"

Sammy looked at me, and I saw that her eyes were filled with tears. "I can't imagine ever being that angry with anyone."

I had to give her that. Still, you heard about it all the time, so some people must have been capable of it. "She didn't say what they were arguing about?"

She shook her head.

"Did she seem scared at all?"

"No." She shook her head again. "She was practically rolling her eyes about it. Like, oh, yeah, Dean's mad again. Whatever, no big deal."

"Does he have a reputation for getting angry?" I looked from Sammy to Rhonda and back. I didn't remember Dean being an angry guy, but there were a lot of years of Cape Bay history that I'd only heard about second hand.

"He has a temper, but I've never heard of him being violent."

"There's a first time for everything," I said, half to myself. This conversation was doing nothing to shake my theory that Dean had been the one to kill Georgina, whether it was premeditated or not.

Before any of us could say anything else, the bell over the café's door jingled, announcing a customer.

Chapter Seven

I looked out through the café to the door to see whether it was an actual customer or a friend who would likely just be joining us in the back to chat. Customers. Two women, one of whom looked vaguely familiar.

I put my down coffee, walked out into the café, and stood behind the counter to take their orders. From the back, I heard the sounds of Sammy and Rhonda getting up from their chairs.

"What can I get for you ladies today?" I tried to sound chipper.

"A latte," the familiar-looking one said. "And none of that fancy milk art stuff. Just give me a normal one, okay?" As soon as the words came out of her mouth, I knew who she was: Diane from yesterday, every bit as abrasive now as she was then. Clearly, it hadn't been her just having an off day.

"Same," the other woman said. "Do you want something to eat?" She glanced at Diane. "I'm hungry."

Diane sighed heavily and looked into our display case. "Two scones."

"I don't want a scone."

She rolled her eyes and looked at the other woman. "Then what do you want?"

The second woman walked around her to look in the display case. "Umm... Uhh..."

"Can you just make our drinks while she makes up her mind?" Diane asked me, although it sounded more like an order than a request.

"Sure thing!" I said with a big smile.

Sammy materialized beside me and grabbed the cups and saucers we'd need. She was pulling the espresso shots before I could even step over to the machine.

"Hello, Diane," Rhonda said.

Diane looked at her. "Rhonda. I forgot you worked here."

There was an awkward silence, and I wondered if there was anyone this woman was nice to.

"I'll have some of those cookies," the second woman said.

Some? I thought. Our cookies were six inches across. People took part of one home more often than one person asked for "some."

"Which kind?" I finally asked.

"The plain ones."

I slid the case open and pointed at the sugar cookies. "These?"

"No, the other ones."

I pointed to the peanut butter cookies, figuring they were the next closest to plain. "These?"

"No! The little ones!"

Little ones? I scanned the contents of the case.

"These!" She poked her stubby-nailed finger at the display case so hard it made a noise.

"Oh, the ladyfingers!"

"Yes." She sounded more than a little disgusted that it had taken me so long to understand. No wonder she hung out with Diane.

"What did you think she meant?" Diane asked.

I took a deep breath and tried not to sound as annoyed as I was with her attitude. "Oh, I was just confused." I forced a smile onto my face and didn't particularly worry myself with whether it was convincing. I pulled on a glove and grabbed a handful of the ladyfingers. A saucer with a paper doily appeared at my elbow, and I dropped the ladyfingers onto it.

Sammy put the saucer on the tray with the lattes and told Diane the price. Diane huffed and puffed like she didn't know we charged for coffee. She dug in her purse for her wallet, pulled out a card, and held it out to Sammy. "That's only for mine. Sabine can pay for her own."

Sabine made a face at Diane's back but started fishing in her purse for her own wallet.

Sammy rung up the two orders then smiled at the women. "If you'll find a seat, Fran will bring your drinks over to you."

The two of them went back to the big table in the corner that the book club had occupied the day before. I watched the drinks on the tray to make sure they didn't spill as I slid the tray off the counter and onto my hand. I had to hold back a smile. As requested, Sammy had left them "normal" with no design poured in. She had, however, poured sloppily with a bit of a heavy hand so that, while not art by any stretch of the mind, a smear of milk appeared across the top of each drink.

I dropped off the drinks and ladyfingers, asked the women if there was anything else I could get them, and went to stand back behind the counter with Sammy and Rhonda. We stood in silence, watching Diane and Sabine, doing our best to make it look as though we weren't.

"Wow," Sammy breathed after a while.

I tried not to laugh, but it was hard. Sammy wasn't usually so critical. But then customers weren't usually so rude, especially not locals who knew they had to live with us for more than a week. We did get tourists once in a while—mostly ones who proudly wore their New York Yankees caps into Boston Red Sox territory—who seemed to think the people of Cape Bay existed only to irritate them on their vacation. Those people did sometimes provoke a reaction from Sammy.

"Yup," Rhonda said.

"Is she always like that?" I asked, barely above a whisper.

"Mm-hmm," Rhonda confirmed.

"It's amazing she has any friends."

"Oh, Sabine's not her friend."

"That explains it. Diane pays her to hang around her."

Rhonda snorted. "No, she's her sister."

I bit my tongue to keep from saying the nasty thing I wanted to. I was supposed to be the boss, after all. I shouldn't encourage snarking about customers, especially not inside the café.

Rhonda looked at me and raised an eyebrow.

"If you can't say anything nice..." I said and mimicked zipping and locking my lips the same way a grade-schooler would.

Rhonda nodded and shot me a knowing smile.

"Everyone has redeeming qualities," Sammy said.

Rhonda and I both looked at her, surprised she was calling us out, but knowing we deserved it all the same.

Sammy flashed the angelic smile that kept the customers coming back. "I have to remind myself sometimes."

Rhonda laughed loud enough that Diane and Sabine looked over at us. I elbowed her, but that just seemed to make her laugh harder. I rolled my eyes, but couldn't help laughing a little along with her. The two of us laughing got Sammy going too, and soon, the three of us had descended into that self-perpetuating giggle fit that only ever happened at the most inopportune times.

I fought to take deep breaths to calm myself down. Slowly, it worked, and I managed to pull myself together. Rhonda's and Sammy's laughing fits ended about the same time—funny how that happens—and the three of us stood there behind the counter, out of breath but happy.

"Oh, I needed that." Sammy's cheeks flushed bright pink, and her blue eyes sparkled.

"Didn't we all?" Rhonda replied.

I knew I did. After thinking so much about Georgina's murder over the past day, a pure giggle fit was exactly what I needed. But then thinking about Georgina reminded me of something I'd wanted to ask Sammy since working in the café for years had led to her knowing pretty much everyone in town and frequently a good bit about them.

"Hey." I lowered my voice even further than it had been when we were talking about Diane and her nasty attitude. Rhonda scooted in next to me so the three of us formed a tight circle. "Do you know anything about Georgina's ex-boyfriend? Alex, I think?" Even if Dean was my prime suspect, I would be stupid not to pursue other leads.

"Yeah. He was actually in here yesterday."

"He was? How did he seem? Was he acting normal?"

"I think so. You talked to him more than I did though."

"I did?"

"Yeah. He came in with some of his coworkers around mid-afternoon. You made his latte."

I thought for a second and realized it was the guy who'd hovered while I made his latte. "The creepy guy?"

"Creepy?" Sammy laughed.

"Well, maybe not creepy, per se, but I don't know, a little too enthusiastic?"

"Yeah, Alex can be a lot."

"Like how?"

Sammy raised an eyebrow. "Why? Do you think he was involved with Georgina's death? I thought you thought Dean did it."

"I do, but Dean told me he thought Alex did it. That's actually partly what made me suspicious of Dean. He was really insistent that I investigate Alex because he said the police weren't going to."

"What makes him think it was Alex?" Rhonda asked.

"He said he was the jealous type. If he couldn't have Georgina, no one would." I watched Sammy as I spoke to see her reaction. She made a face like she was confused or thinking. "Do you know him well enough to know if that sounds like him?"

"Well…" she said slowly. "Like I said, he can be a lot, but…"

I waited for her to put her thoughts together.

Rhonda didn't. "Spit it out!"

"Well, they broke up kind of a while ago."

"That doesn't mean he was over her."

"I know, I just—I hadn't heard her talk about him too much lately. I know back when they were together, things could get pretty intense—"

"Intense like how?" I interrupted.

"They fought, I think. But I think that's why they broke up. They were fighting all the time."

It was the reason a lot of couples broke up. But one party of a lot of couples didn't end up dead a few months later. "Did he ever get violent?"

Sammy shook her head quickly. "No. Not that I ever heard. They both had strong personalities, and I think they clashed sometimes. Maybe a lot of times."

Nothing Sammy said really conflicted with what Dean had said. She didn't make Alex out to be a killer though. Of course, Sammy gave everybody the benefit of the doubt. If she was on a jury, she'd probably want DNA evidence, eyewitnesses, video footage, and testimony from the defendant's mother that the man on trial was her son before she'd convict anyone because there was always a possibility of mistaken identity. I wondered if maybe I needed to look into Alex a little more—not that I wasn't still suspicious of Dean.

I noticed Rhonda staring at me. "What?" I asked.

"Just trying to figure out if you suspect Alex now."

"I..." I hesitated, not even sure of what I thought. "It would be premature to rule anyone out."

Rhonda laughed. "You sound like you're on a detective show. You've been watching them to pick up tips on how to investigate a murder, haven't you?"

"Nooo," I replied, drawing the word out and putting a faux-innocent look on my face. Then I laughed. "No, I'm kidding. But I've probably watched enough of them in my life to have picked up a thing or two without even trying."

"You don't fool me," Rhonda said with her eyes narrowed but twinkling. "I know you're studying."

Sammy giggled, Rhonda laughed, then I covered my mouth to keep my own laugh from coming out. All we needed was to kick off another giggle fit.

Hysterical laughter averted, Rhonda brought the conversation back to my investigation of Georgina's murder. "When are you getting back out there to do some interrogating?"

"I don't interrogate."

"Fran's too kind and polite to interrogate," Sammy said. "She 'talks to' or 'has a chat with.'"

"Like my kids' teachers do with me when one of the boys hasn't been doing his homework," Rhonda said.

"Exactly!" Sammy laughed.

Rhonda laughed with her and looked quickly over at me in a way that made me laugh. "But seriously, when are you getting back to investigating? You have a romantic Italian vacation to leave for in less than a week. You need to get a move on."

"I was thinking I'd try to track down Dean again tomorrow morning before I come in here."

"Tomorrow? You don't think you'll be able to talk to him today? Or Alex?" Sammy sounded concerned.

I felt for her. Georgina had been her friend, and I suspected she felt like she might have missed a warning sign, either when Georgina talked about arguing with Dean, or maybe even before that, when she talked about arguing with Alex.

"Well, I'll be here all afternoon, but I might be able to go talk to Dean again right after I close up." I paused, remembering that it had been unusual to see the lights on down at Howard Jewelers at closing time. I'd have to track him down at home or something. Of course, he'd asked me to look into the case, so he shouldn't be surprised to hear from me. Maybe I could call over to the shop during the day and make arrangements to see him.

"Just go this afternoon." Rhonda interrupted my thoughts.

"I can't just leave the café unattended! And don't suggest just closing it down for a few hours like you did for the team-building shopping spree you want us to take. I definitely can't shut it down twice in a week."

"No, don't shut it down. Why would you shut it down?"

"Because no one will be here if I leave? Sammy's due to leave soon. I can't ask her to stay."

Rhonda looked at me like I was hopelessly confused. "But I'm here. I can stay a while if I have to. The boys can either wait to eat or fix something themselves. They're not infants."

"The boys?" Sammy asked. "Where's Dan?"

Rhonda waved her hand dismissively at the mention of her husband. "Oh, he's one of the boys. When it comes to the cooking and cleaning, I lump him in with them." She rolled her eyes dramatically then gave me and Sammy a pointed look, apparently ready to dole out some life advice. "Don't ever let yourself get outnumbered. Three of them and one of me. Why couldn't I have had just one girl? Then we'd at least be even."

I waited a few seconds to let her have her moment, then tried to bring the conversation back around to Rhonda manning the café for the afternoon. "Are you sure you don't mind if I go out for a little while?"

Now that I potentially had a way of doing it, I was a little excited about the prospect of digging into the new information I'd gotten from Sammy.

"Yeah, absolutely! It'll be good practice for the next couple weeks. Ease me into it before I'm really on my own."

"You won't be on your own!" Sammy said. "I'll be here!"

"You can't be here all the time!" Rhonda retorted.

"Well, I'm not going to leave you here alone if you don't feel like you can handle it!"

"Are you saying you don't think I can handle it?" Rhonda asked. I could tell that she was messing with Sammy, but by the look on Sammy's face, I didn't think Sammy could.

"No! I just mean sometimes, it gets really busy, and it's hard for one person to handle, and I don't want you to think I'm going to abandon you!"

"Sammy, I'm joking," Rhonda said, and a look of relief came across Sammy's face. "I know you'd never leave me here to struggle." She turned to me. "But you—you should go find Alex. Or Dean. Or anyone else who's ever been known to argue with Georgina. I'll stay here with the two of them"—she nodded at Diane and Sabine, who were huddled over their normal lattes, seeming to be trying to keep their conversation as private and quiet as we had—"and whoever else comes in. If things get hectic, I'll turn on the bat signal, and you can come rescue me."

I looked at Sammy, who shrugged. "If you say so." I went to the back to take off my apron.

Chapter Eight

Ten minutes later, I stood outside of Howard Jewelers for the second time in two days, after having only been inside maybe twice before in my lifetime. I vaguely remembered coming once with my mom when I was in high school when she wanted to get a ring resized, and I felt like I'd been there another time, but I wasn't sure. It was funny how a place could be as familiar a part of the landscape as Howard Jewelers was to me without actually me having all that much direct experience with it.

The side window that the brick had been thrown through was still boarded up, and the sign in the door still said, "Closed," as I expected it would for at least a few more days. Even after the police declared that the shop was no longer a crime scene—which the crime scene tape over the door and the plywood in the window told me they hadn't—Dean would have to have the glass in the window and the display case replaced and probably the carpet as well. Then he'd probably have to jump through some hoops for the insurance company—putting bars over those giant plate-glass windows, I guessed—before he could restock the cases and reopen. I didn't envy him.

I didn't see any signs of life inside the shop, so I went around the back in hopes that Dean's car would be there again. It was. I pushed the buzzer and looked up into the camera again. He answered the door more quickly this time.

"Hi Fran!" He smiled. He looked better today. He wore a striped button-down shirt tucked into black pants, and his hair was slicked back. "I didn't expect to see you so soon! You haven't changed your mind about helping me, have you?"

"No, I haven't changed my mind about helping *Georgina*." I wanted to leave no doubt in his mind that I was doing this for her, not for him.

"Great," he said without noticing the distinction. "Do you have news for me? Did you talk to her ex-boyfriend?"

He looked at me expectantly and seemed to realize that he hadn't invited me in, and perhaps it was rude not to when you were asking someone to solve the murder of one of your employees. "Do you want to come in? So we can talk in private?" He glanced around the deserted back alley like someone might have been lurking, hoping to overhear something important. It seemed to me like the behavior of someone with a guilty conscience.

"That would be great." I tried to sound as friendly and personable as I could.

Dean stepped aside and held the door open for me. The back room of the jewelry store was neater than it had been the day before. The boxes were stacked more neatly and seemed to have some sort of organization to them. I sat down on the couch under the stairs. It had been cleaned off except for a pillow and blanket piled up at one end. I wondered if Dean had slept there the night before. *He must be pretty brave to sleep there the night after a murder and robbery. Brave or guilty.*

Dean pulled a rolling chair over so it faced where I sat on the couch and planted himself down on it. It bounced a little as it adjusted to his weight. "So did you talk to her ex? What do you think? Did you see what I mean about him being possessive?" He leaned forward as he fired his questions at me.

"No, I haven't talked to him yet."

Dean leaned back with something that might have been a scowl on his face. "You haven't? Then what are you doing here? Shouldn't you be out talking to him?"

"I think he's at work, Dean. He works an office job, right?"

He relaxed a little. "Yeah, I think he does. Some kind of internet start-up or something."

"An internet start-up? Here? In Cape Bay?" Cape Bay was one of the last places I would have expected someone to locate their start-up. Somewhere without internet was about the only place I could imagine being less likely.

"Isn't the point of the internet that you can work from anywhere?"

"I guess so." I started to tell Dean I had some more questions for him, but he spoke before I could get anything out.

"Yeah, they're in an office up above one of the shops here on Main Street. I can't remember which one it is, but I'm sure you can find out."

"It shouldn't be too hard—"

"I don't know for sure, but I think he rented that space so it would be easier to keep an eye on her when she was working. They only moved in a couple of months ago. It was definitely after the break-up. You know, he came in here a couple of times a week, bothering her. It was as if he couldn't let her go, like he just had to be near her. He was always in her space too, getting close to her. Even when she'd try to walk away, he'd follow her."

"Had he been in recently?" I asked quickly before he had the chance to start talking again.

Dean froze for a second. "Uh, no, I don't think so. But I mean, I'm not here all the time, so there were lots of times he could have come by without me seeing him."

"Did Georgina mention him coming in?"

"Uh, no, but she knew how I felt about it. She probably didn't mention it because she knew I didn't like it."

"Did you ever see him get violent with her?"

"No, but why would he do that if I was right there? I mean, that's just asking for trouble, isn't it?"

He puffed out his chest and tried to make himself look bigger than he actually was. He wasn't exactly small, but he wasn't a big man either. He struck me as the kind of guy who worked out enough to say that he did but not nearly enough to give him an impressive physique. I wasn't sure that the muscles he did have were enough to scare much of anyone out of fighting him, even if they were the tall and skinny type I seemed to remember Alex being. Of course, I didn't want to fight him or anyone else, so I wasn't really sure I was a great judge of whether a grown man would be afraid to fight Dean.

I just smiled at him. "Yeah, probably."

Dean hadn't done much in the conversation so far to put me off my theory that he had killed Georgina. He'd admitted he hadn't seen Alex around Georgina recently and that he'd never seen him get violent.

Neither of those things meant that Alex couldn't have killed her, but they also didn't make Alex look like a more likely killer than Dean. At least I knew more or less where to find Alex now since I did want to talk to him, whether he was my prime suspect or not. He might even know something more about the arguments Sammy told me Georgina had been having with Dean, which reminded me that I should ask him about that.

I made a show of hesitating and looking uncomfortable before asking so that he didn't think I was grilling him. "Dean? Can I ask you an awkward question?"

He stared at me for an uncomfortably long few seconds before answering. "I guess so." He crossed his arms over his chest.

"I heard that you and Georgina had gotten into some arguments lately. What were those about?"

"Geez, you sound like the cops!"

"I do?"

"Yeah, they were in here again this morning. Apparently, since the damn ring didn't show up in a pawn shop within twenty-four hours, they think I staged the robbery for the insurance money and killed her in the process."

Well, at least my theory wasn't totally off base. And it sounded as though the police had heard about Georgina and Dean's arguments too. I wondered if they had also thought of the possibility that Dean had killed Georgina in a rage and then staged the robbery for the insurance claim.

"What about the arguments, Dean?" I asked quietly. I tried to put concern in my voice and hoped he would interpret it as concern for his continued status as a free citizen.

He shifted in his chair. The wheels wiggled, shifting him back and forth an inch or so. "We just had some disagreements about how things should work at the store."

"It's your store though, Dean."

"I know! That's why I—" He stopped and shook his head. "I'm happy to take requests from my employees, but I don't like it when they do things behind my back, that's all."

"Georgina did something behind your back?"

He got a squirrely look on his face again. "Well, no, I mean, yes. It wasn't anything really major. I probably would have been fine with it. I just would have liked her to tell me before she went and did it."

Even if I couldn't imagine getting into a shouting match with one of my employees over something at the café, I knew I wouldn't be happy if one of them went behind my back on something. It was the principle. "What did she do?" I asked, thinking it may be important, or at least relevant, especially if it had something to do with the security protocols.

"I said it wasn't anything major. I just wished she'd talked to me about it first."

"But what was it?"

"Nothing important."

"It was important enough to you that you argued with her about it."

"I overreacted, okay? It wasn't a big deal."

The more he argued about it, the more I was convinced that he was hiding something. A motive for murder? I needed to find another angle to approach it from.

"Dean, if you want me to help Georgina—help you—you have to help me, especially now that the police are looking at you for her murder. It doesn't matter how guilty

Alex looks if you look guiltier. You have to tell me."

Dean squinted as he looked at me. I suspected he was trying to determine if he should trust me. Eventually, he sighed and shook his head. He slumped in his chair a little. "She rearranged some of the jewelry in the displays."

Was that all? They got into a screaming match over some rearranged merchandise? Maybe Dean was wound tighter than I thought. Unless... "Did that include the ring that was stolen?"

"What? No. Um..." He paused for a second and seemed to think. "No, not the ring. The ring's always been in the back corner it was stolen from. People came in to see it. I wanted them to walk past everything else we had on the way in and out. Get them coming and going, you know? They see everything we sell on the way in, then they see the ring, they want it, but they can't have it, so, maybe they buy themselves a little something else that's more in their price range."

"Did that happen often?" I had trouble believing all that many people really came in to see the ring, but I wasn't going to argue.

He shrugged. "Often enough."

I sighed. I had to think of what to ask next. *Where were you that night? Did you kill her accidentally or on purpose? Why did the alarm company call you instead of the police?*

"Why did the alarm company call you instead of the police?" I asked.

"What?"

"When the brick went through the window, why did the alarm company call you instead of the police? My alarm company calls the police."

"How do you know about that?"

"That my alarm company calls the police? It's in my contract. They'd better call the police." I wondered if I should set off my alarm one night as a test.

"No, that they called me when the alarm went off."

"Oh, Susan told me." Dean looked confused, so I explained. "Susan... I don't know her last name. She's a customer. She's the one who told me that Georgina died. She heard about it from someone at the police department." I could have told him it was Margaret Robbins, the receptionist, but I thought it was best to keep some information to myself.

Dean relaxed a little but still seemed to be on edge. I wondered if I'd hit on something important. "We'd had a few false alarms recently. If you get too many, the cops start fining you. I told the alarm company to call me, and I'd call the police if it was real. I can't afford the fines, and I don't want to get on the cops' bad side."

It seemed to make sense. But the false alarms were at least something I could verify with my contacts at the police department: Ryan and his boss, Detective Mike Stanton. I realized that I hadn't seen Mike since Georgina died. I wondered what he'd have to say about my investigation. He was never too enthusiastic about me getting involved with police business. He never really tried to stop me either though.

I brought my mind back to Dean. I didn't know what else to ask him without giving away my suspicions. I went with the most neutral question I could think of. "Have you thought of anything else I should know? Anyone else who might have had a motive to kill Georgina or to rob you?"

"You don't believe me that it was Alex? Trust me. It was him. Go talk to him, and you'll understand."

"Okay, I will." I stood up. At least for today, I was done talking to Dean.

"Good. Come see me again after you've talked to him."

I didn't like the implication that I was working for him, but I smiled. "I will."

I was halfway out the door when I thought of something and turned around. "Do you have a picture of the ring? I just realized I don't even know what it looks like."

Dean's eyes lit up. "Of course I have a picture!" He went over to the box-covered desk and shifted things around. After several seconds, he extracted a sheet of paper and brought it over. "It's blown up, of course, but the scale is right there." He turned the picture around for me to see.

I gasped. It was exquisite, heirloom quality, all the enthusiastic adjectives Dean had used when he described it to me the night before. There was a large oval diamond in the center, surrounded by two rows of bead-set diamonds. To top it off, the band was encrusted with diamonds. It would have been more at home on display at

Tiffany's in New York than it was at Howard Jewelers in Cape Bay. I suddenly believed that people came in just to look at it.

"Two and a half carats," Dean said. "Completely flawless. Even the little ones."

"It's stunning," I breathed.

"You see why I couldn't give it up?"

I nodded. "Are you sure someone wouldn't steal it just because they wanted to have it? I mean, it's amazing."

"Fat chance. If someone stole this, it would be for the money."

I stared at the picture for a few more seconds. I didn't think he was wrong. The insurance money you'd get for that being stolen could certainly be an incentive—maybe even to kill.

Chapter Nine

I was deep in thought the whole way back to the café. My brain swirled with everything Dean had said, the way he'd said it, and what it could mean. I still felt like he was trying a little too hard to convince me of Alex's guilt. There was something more that he wasn't telling me; I just didn't know what it was. I had so many questions. There were so many things I didn't know.

I needed to know more about Alex and his relationship with Georgina. Dean made it sound as if Alex was a jealousy-crazed lunatic who was more than capable of murder. Sammy made it sound like he was the kind of guy who might come on a little strong but ultimately wasn't any more dangerous than anyone else. It was possible that they were both versions of the truth, but only one of them could be right about whether he was the murderer.

And then there was Dean. In addition to all the money he'd be making off the ring disappearing in a theft, there was the fact that he'd been arguing with Georgina over something as insignificant as the arrangement of the display cases. Was Dean a hothead, or was Georgina overstepping her bounds that much? Was the ring's apparent theft the cause of Georgina's death, or a happy—for Dean—side effect? Or had he maybe seen a way to kill two birds with one stone, one of them literally?

I wondered if I was overlooking any other suspects. I hadn't even been on the case for twenty-four hours. Was it too soon to feel so strongly about the likely culprit, or was I just demonstrating what Diane had said about finding a suspect in the first forty-eight hours?

And when was I going to pack for Italy? It was already Wednesday, and we were leaving on Tuesday. I didn't even know if I had everything I needed. And if I didn't, when was I going to go shopping? I considered actually taking Rhonda up on her shopping trip offer, which brought its own host of problems.

By the time I got back to the café, I had a million questions on my mind, and I didn't think I could have made a decision about even one of them if my life depended on it. I pulled open the door and walked in, barely glancing around at the tables to see how busy it was. Rhonda was there, and I was sure she had everything under control.

I was three steps from the back room when she called out to me.

"Fran!" She stepped toward me with her hand out to grab my arm if she needed to.

I stopped and looked at her with what I'm sure was a pitiful look. I really hoped she wasn't going to ask me anything more complicated than "Where are the napkins?" And I wasn't sure I could even manage an answer to that. But it turned out she didn't have a question at all, which should have been a relief.

"There's someone here to see you. In the back."

I looked at her, not sure what kind of reaction to have. It was like when someone said, "Guess what?" without giving you any clue what you were supposed to be guessing.

"I didn't want you to be startled." She dropped her hand and gave me a half smile.

Well, that didn't sound good. I took a deep breath and walked into the back room to see who it was.

"Hi, Franny. I've been waiting for you." He sat in the desk chair, holding his standard complimentary to-go cup of coffee in one hand. The chair was turned so he couldn't miss me walking in the door, and I couldn't miss him. His suit jacket was unbuttoned, and he looked pretty comfortable sitting there with one ankle crossed over his knee.

"So I see. How're you doing, Mike?" I couldn't say I was surprised to see Detective Mike Stanton of the Cape Bay Police Department sitting in my office, especially since I'd just been thinking about how I hadn't seen him yet. I wasn't exactly excited about the conversation, but it could have been worse.

"I'm doing well enough, considering the circumstances. Have a seat, why don't you? And shut the door while you're at it."

It felt weird being ordered around in my own shop, but I did as I was told. "How're Sandra and the kids?"

I knew he hadn't come on a social call, but I didn't think that was any reason not to be friendly. Besides, we'd grown up together, and the only reason we weren't friendlier was that I kept nosing around his official investigations, which he didn't appreciate too much. I did have it on good authority, though, that his objection was mostly perfunctory, based on his general belief that citizens should stay out of things and let the police do their job.

"They're good." He took a sip of his coffee. I could see the steam still coming out of it, so he must not have been waiting too long. "Kids are growing up fast." I saw the corners of his eyes crinkle up in a slight smile.

"How old are they now?"

"Six and eight." The pride was obvious in his voice.

"Playing any sports?"

"My little guy's playing football—flag, not tackle. Sandra'd never let him play tackle." He chuckled a little. "My girl's all dance all the time. She'd wear a leotard and tights to school every day if we'd let her. We tried to sign her up for soccer a couple years ago, but she cried through every practice until I couldn't take it anymore and told Sandra we had to let her quit. She wants to be a ballerina when she grows up. Her teacher says she's got natural talent, so we'll see."

It was sweet seeing big, tough Mike go all soft talking about his kids.

"But I didn't come here to talk about my kids, did I?" He shifted in his chair and raised his eyebrows at me.

"Well, I don't know, Mike. Maybe you did. Nothing wrong with coming by to have a chat with an old friend." I smiled at him. I knew that wasn't why he was there, and he knew that I knew. But I couldn't let him off the hook that easy.

"Well, no, there's not. But it's not why I'm here." He smiled benevolently.

"No?"

He shook his head and took another sip of his coffee. "You know it's not."

I laughed and shrugged. "Well, I wasn't going to volunteer for the Inquisition."

"Fair enough." He looked at me for a few seconds, presumably waiting to see if I was going to volunteer anything. Of course, I wasn't, so eventually he gave in. "So you were down at Howard Jewelers talking to Dean just now? Presumably about the Rockwell murder?"

"How do you know that? Did Rhonda tell on me?"

He shook his head. "No, I saw you go in."

"You did?"

He nodded.

"How?"

"I was watching the place, keeping up with who was coming and going."

So Dean hadn't been totally off base looking around for people spying on him. "Where were you hiding?"

He smirked. "Well, if I told you, it wouldn't be a very good hiding spot anymore, would it?"

"I guess not. Since you already know, yes, I was talking to Dean. About Georgina's murder."

"Murder, eh? So you don't think it was accidental?"

"You just called it a murder!"

"Did I? Huh. Must need more caffeine." He took a big swig from his cup. It had clearly cooled off pretty significantly since he didn't even flinch. Either that or it was a technique he'd honed over years of police work to intimidate the criminals he was investigating—not that that would have surprised me with Mike.

"Besides, isn't it considered a murder whether or not it was an accident if it happened during a robbery?"

"Yup. Felony murder." He took another swallow of his coffee. "So you were talking to Dean about Georgina's murder?"

"Yup."

"Does that mean I have a civilian trying to work my murder case again?"

"Well, I wouldn't say I'm trying to work it."

"What would you say then?"

I thought for a moment and decided to apply my best PR spin to it. "I'm reaching out to my fellow citizens who have been affected by the recent tragedy of Georgina Rockwell's apparent murder so that we can discuss our thoughts and feelings in an effort to understand the event."

Mike gave me a look that seemed to be a cross between skeptical and amused. Then he sighed and put his coffee cup down on the table. He uncrossed his legs and leaned forward, resting his elbows on his knees. He folded his hands in front of him.

"Listen, Fran..." I swallowed hard in dread. "If what you're doing is talking to people to comfort yourself or to satisfy your own curiosity, that's fine. As long as you don't interfere in my investigation—you don't damage or destroy or plant any evidence or try to affect what anyone says to me—I don't care what you do. But this is the thing. You are a private citizen, acting on your own without any encouragement or direction from me or anyone else in the police department. If you become aware of some piece of information that may be relevant to my investigation, I expect you to bring it to me, as I would expect any private citizen to do. But—and I can't stress this enough—" He paused and looked into my eyes. He had brought his pointer fingers together and was using them to emphasize his point. "You are not an agent of the police, nor are you acting as one. If you were working for me—even if you weren't a sworn law enforcement officer—you would be bound by all the rules of law that bind me. If you did anything that violated those laws, anything that came out of it would be thrown out in court. It could completely torpedo my case. So I'm telling you this again. You are not working for me, and under no circumstances are you to suggest to anyone that you are. Do you understand?"

I nodded, a little intimidated by the intensity of his speech.

"Please say it out loud."

"I understand."

"As long as you don't go breaking any laws or getting in my way, you're a private citizen, and there's nothing I can do to stop you from talking to whoever you want. And honestly, you probably wouldn't listen if I told you to mind your own business, would you?"

I couldn't help smiling. "Probably not."

"That's what I thought." He leaned back in his chair and picked his coffee back up. "Moral of the story: don't screw up my investigation. Don't get any ideas in your head that you're working for me. But if you find anything out, don't keep it from me. Got it?"

"Got it."

"Good." He stood up and shoved his coffee-free hand into his pocket. "So are we good? You got any questions for me?

You haven't already solved the case, have you?"

I thought for a second, partly to consider whether I'd learned anything worth telling and partly to screw with Mike. "Nope." He started for the door, but I stopped him. "You're not just looking at this as a robbery, right? You're considering the possibility that someone wanted to kill Georgina?"

"Of course. This isn't my first week on the job, Fran."

"Okay, good. I just wanted to make sure."

He eyed me. "Why? Have you heard something?"

"Dean thinks her ex-boyfriend, Alex something, may have come after her."

"Yeah, he mentioned that."

"And you're looking into it?"

"Like I said, it's not my first week on the job."

"Thanks."

"Anything else?"

"Nope, not today."

"I'll see you around then." He headed again for the door. "I'd say, *'bon voyage,'* but I have a feeling I'll be seeing you again before you and Matt head out of town."

"As much of my coffee as you drink, you're probably right."

"You got me there." He wiggled his cup in his hand before opening the door. "Hey, Rhonda! I get free refills, right?"

"Sure do!" Rhonda called back.

"All your drinks are free, Mike," I said to his back. It had been my family's policy since my grandparents first opened Antonia's: police and fire eat free.

"And I appreciate that," I heard him say. Then he must have gone over to the display case because he was out of my line of sight and talking about food. "You got anything new I should try? I didn't have much for lunch."

"Monica brought over a fresh batch of ladyfingers this morning," Rhonda said.

"Do I look like the kind of man who eats something called ladyfingers? I'll have a piece of tiramisu."

"You know there are ladyfingers in tiramisu, right, Mike?"

"Don't ruin it for me."

I shook my head and walked over to the chair Mike had just vacated. I sat down and drummed my fingers on the desk for a minute then grabbed a piece of paper and a pen. I needed to make a list of everything I was thinking about Georgina's murder and my vacation. Two incredibly different subjects, but I wasn't going to get anything done on either of them if I didn't get organized.

I scribbled down all the questions that had run through my mind on my walk back to the café after talking to Dean and then made notes about what I'd learned so far. When I looked at it, it didn't look like much. I was working on a hunch and a couple of conversations with someone who quite possibly had every reason in the world to lie to me. It wasn't nearly enough to either satisfy my curiosity or consider the case solved.

I tried to start thinking about what I needed to do next and who I needed to talk to, but my mind kept flitting to my Italy trip and everything I had to do to get ready for it. Deciding I was never going to make any progress unless I cleared my mind, I grabbed a second sheet of paper and started making a list of everything I had to do before leaving for Italy. I knew I wasn't going to remember everything–no matter how organized I thought I was, at the last minute, I always realized I'd forgotten something like shampoo or deodorant or shoes–but at least having a list would make me feel a little less scatterbrained.

When I'd written down every last thing I could think of, including things like checking the weather and making sure the next supply order was placed for the café, I pushed the piece of paper aside and sat back in my chair. I looked at my notes on Georgina's death and realized what I needed to do next.

Chapter Ten

I sat for a minute and listened to the noises coming from the café. It sounded pretty quiet. "Hey, Rhonda?"

After a few seconds, she appeared in the doorway. "What's up?"

"Who's that other girl who works over at Howard Jewelers?"

"Which one? There are a couple, and I think a guy. And then I think another guy."

"The main one. You know, the blonde."

"The tall blonde or the short blonde?"

She seemed average height to me. "The bleached blonde."

"They're both bleached blondes."

I rolled my eyes. Rhonda's face was completely impassive. Knowing her, there was every chance she was messing with me, but I couldn't tell. "The obvious bleached blonde."

"Karen." She smiled, and I knew she'd been drawing it out at least a little.

"Do you know how to get a hold of her? Where she lives or anything?"

Rhonda thought for a second then shook her head. "I know she lives in town somewhere, but I'm not sure where. I've seen her with her dog in the park, though, when I pick the boys up from school." She looked at the clock over the door. "Usually about now."

I jumped up out of my chair and reached for my purse in the desk drawer before I stopped and looked at Rhonda.

Before I could even say anything, she waved me off. "Go. I can take care of things here."

"Thanks, Rhonda!" I grabbed my purse and looked around to see if there was anything else I needed before I left. I spotted my notes on the table and picked them up. I folded them and put them in my bag. "Are you okay closing up if I don't make it back in time? I mean, I'll be back if I can, but—"

"Go where the investigation takes you. Don't worry about me. I can always call if I run into any issues."

"Thanks a million!" I dashed out the back door. If Rhonda usually saw Karen at the park about this time, I needed to hurry. I didn't want to just walk up and start grilling her out of the blue. But Rhonda had given me the in I needed, and it was time for Latte's walk anyway.

It wasn't far from the café back to my house, even without taking the shortcut through my neighbors' backyards that I'd taken as a child. I'd taken that route once since I'd been back in town, and I still hadn't recovered enough from the unpleasant surprise I'd found there to try it again, so I kept to the streets and the sidewalks.

I turned onto my quiet street. A few of my retiree neighbors were out, tending to their gardens. I'd known most of them my entire life. They waved a greeting, and I waved back but hurried on toward my house. I knew I was developing a bit of a reputation for being an uppity New Yorker who wouldn't stop and chat, but today wasn't the day to remedy that.

I unlocked my front door and pushed it open. "Latte!"

Even though it was more or less the same time I always came home to let him out, it took him a few seconds to rouse from his nap—right on top of my pillow, based on the collection of dog hair I found there every evening—and bound down the stairs.

He pranced around my feet while I tried to get my hands in the same place as his collar so that I could put his leash on. Every time I got close to hooking the leash, he darted for the door like he thought I'd already done it. I was used to the game, and it didn't usually bother me, but today, I was anxious to get to the park so I could catch Karen and talk to her—if she was even there. The frustration was getting to me. "Latte! Sit still!"

Apparently, the obedience lessons I'd been trying to give him were actually paying off because he plopped his bottom down on the floor and immediately raised one paw for the "shake" that usually came next.

"Well, why didn't I try that sooner?" I muttered, bending down and finally getting the leash on him.

I grabbed his favorite tennis ball then led him outside and locked the door behind us. Even after the recent spate of murders, I was unusual among the denizens of Cape Bay for religiously locking my house and car. When I'd first moved away, locking up had seemed odd to me, but now I couldn't imagine not doing it. It wasn't that I expected to be murdered in my home, but it only took a second, and it gave me some peace of mind, especially since I was apparently known around town for sussing out murderers. I didn't know whose bad side I might be getting on.

Latte didn't mind my quick pace down the sidewalk, even though it was much faster than our usual speed. He trotted along, tongue out, looking like the happiest dog in the world. It wasn't long before we got to the park. We came in through the back entrance. I didn't see Karen anywhere, but if Rhonda could see her on her drive, she'd have to be at the front of the park.

Latte resisted a little when we didn't stop at the soccer fields where we normally played, but stayed by my side as we passed the playground and the pond and then went up the stairs where we'd first found each other when he was a stray, and I had just stumbled into my first murder investigation.

As soon as we crested the stairs, I saw Karen and her big red Irish setter, openly flouting our annoying, relatively new leash law. In general, nobody in Cape Bay cared if you threw a ball for your dog in the park, but someone moved into town and campaigned the town council to stop such reckless behavior by dog owners.

Karen wasn't the only person who didn't care. While a lot of people were like me and just used the enclosed soccer fields as a makeshift dog park, I still saw quite a few people acting as if the law didn't exist and playing fetch with their dogs elsewhere in the park. I was also pretty sure the police didn't care and not only because they'd been keeping busy lately investigating murders.

I tried to look nonchalant as I walked over. "Hey! It's Karen, right?"

She nodded, her platinum hair catching the sun. It was impressively shiny for being so heavily processed. If I didn't know better, I would have almost thought it was natural except for the streak of dark roots along her part. Her whole look was like that, though. From far away, she looked like she was nineteen or twenty. Up close, I couldn't tell whether she was closer to thirty or forty, but I knew she'd definitely been old enough to drink for more than a few years.

Her tastefully distressed jeans looked like they were feeling a little extra distressed by how tight they were. She had them tucked into a knee-high pair of high-heeled boots that I might have worn on the pavement in New York City, but wouldn't have risked in a grassy field in Cape Bay. I could see myself going down hard and probably breaking a bone. Karen was either gifted with exceptional balance, exceptional courage, or exceptional stupidity to play with her dog in them. Her shirt was long sleeved in a concession to the chill creeping into the fall air, but it had a low scoop neck, and the hem just barely brushed the top of her jeans. I had a feeling that there was more than one way she could bend and end up showing off the goods.

She squinted her heavily lined and mascaraed eyes at me. "Antonia?"

"Francesca," I corrected her. I wasn't surprised by her mistake. It was a common one. There were even a few people who insisted on calling me Antonia even after I'd corrected them several times. "Antonia was my grandmother."

"That's right. I couldn't remember if it was named after your mom's mom or daughter." She stuck out her manicured hand. "Nice to meet you."

"You too." I switched Latte's tennis ball into my leash hand and shook her hand.

"And sorry about your mom."

"Thanks. Sorry about Georgina." I was surprised to have gotten to the subject of Georgina so easily. I'd expected to make dog-based small talk for a while: what's his name, his breed, how old is he? It was the dog version of the questions parents ask each other while they watched their kids at the park. We only had to stop chatting slightly less often to yell at our charges to behave.

"Thanks. I still can't believe it." She held out her hand, and her dog plopped his tennis ball into it. She hurled it back across the park, and her dog took off after it. Latte jerked to the end of his leash, looking enviously at the ball. Karen looked down at him and then at the tennis ball in my hand. "It'll probably work if we alternate."

I hesitated for a second. I generally preferred to follow the rules, and letting Latte off his leash was obviously against them. Still, I wouldn't be able to get any information from Karen if I didn't make nice with her. I bent down and unhooked Latte. When Karen's Irish setter picked up his ball and headed back our way, I tossed Latte's ball out as far as I could. I thought for a second that the setter was going to drop his ball and go after Latte's, but apparently, he decided to stick with the treasure he had and kept loping back toward us. Latte took off to get his prize.

"Do you know if the police have any leads?" I hoped she wouldn't mind me keeping the conversation on Georgina.

She shrugged as she threw the ball. "I dunno. But Dean sure seems to think Georgina's ex did it. He kept going on about it when he called to tell me what happened."

At least he was consistent with his story. Maybe he figured that the more people he told, the more believable it would be. "Do you think he killed her?" I took the drooly ball from Latte and waited until the setter turned back toward us to throw it.

She looked at me for a second. "Alex?" She shrugged and shook her head a little. "I dunno. A brick seems like a weird murder weapon." She threw her ball.

"But it *was* the murder weapon, wasn't it?" I took the ball from Latte.

"Well, yeah, I mean, it just seems like a weird choice. Like, if you were going to murder someone, why would you pick a *brick*? I mean, a gun, a knife, poison, I don't know, strangling. Of all the things you could pick, why would you pick a *brick*? It seems easy to screw up."

I threw Latte's ball while I thought about what she said. She had a point. If Alex—or Dean—was planning to kill Georgina, why wouldn't they choose a more foolproof weapon? It wasn't as if they could have thrown the brick through the window over and over until they got it right. Maybe the police were right about it being a robbery after all. But I still didn't think that eliminated Dean. He could have been staging the robbery to get the insurance money and accidentally killed Georgina in the process.

"If you ask me, it was a straight-up robbery," she said, tossing her dog's ball. "As soon as I heard that all they took was that ring, it was obvious."

"Really? Dean said he didn't think it was a robbery because that was all they took."

She arched an immaculately plucked and heavily penciled eyebrow at me. "You talked to Dean?"

"Well, yeah, you know." I stumbled for words. Karen's dog had just turned around and started running in our direction, so I hurled Latte's ball again in an attempt to stall for time. As Latte took off, it came to me. "My coffee shop's on Main Street too. It's scary to think about. What if it had been Antonia's instead of Howard's?"

"Last time I checked, Antonia's sells cappuccinos and cupcakes, not expensive diamond rings."

"Tiramisu too!" The business owner in me was unable to resist an opportunity to promote our offerings. "And ladyfingers now. They're the same ones used in the tiramisu, and they're delicious. You should come in sometime and have some. If you get a latte with them and dip the ladyfingers in it? Oh! So good!"

She looked at me like I'd lost my mind then nodded slowly. "I'll keep that in mind." She tossed her dog's ball across the grass.

"So, um, you said something about knowing it was a robbery as soon as you heard that only the ring was stolen?"

"Yeah."

"How did you know?" I threw Latte's ball, trying to look casual, as her dog headed back toward us.

"Because I knew who did it."

Chapter Eleven

"You knew who did it?" I bit my tongue to keep from asking why Karen had gone on about Dean's theory about Georgina's murder instead of saying immediately that she knew who did it.

"Yeah." She held on to her Irish setter's ball while she waited for Latte to run back toward us, his drool-soaked tennis ball grasped in his teeth.

"Who?" I asked, afraid she wasn't going to offer it up.

"Guy named Sean Donnelly. He's the janitor over at the high school."

"How did you know?"

"He'd been in a bunch of times, asking about the ring. Apparently, his girlfriend said she wouldn't marry him unless he got it for her."

"Wait, did you say he's the janitor at the high school?"

She laughed derisively as she hurled the dog's ball again. "Yeah."

"But the ring cost fifty thousand dollars."

"Yeah, no kidding."

"Did she not actually want to marry him?" I threw Latte's ball.

"As far as I know, she did. She's just one of those entitled types who think she deserves nothing short of the very best, and if a guy wants to marry her, he'd better provide the most amazing engagement ring known to man."

"Do high school janitors get paid a lot more than I think?"

"No, they don't. Sean doesn't, anyway. He came in a bunch of times to try to negotiate and get the price down or work out a payment plan, but I don't think he could have afforded the cheapest ring in the store, let alone that thing."

"And you think he wanted it bad enough to break in and steal it?"

"I think his girlfriend wanted it enough for him to do it. He would get really intense and kind of desperate seeming. It's not that I expected him to break in and take it, but if it was him, I can't say I'd be surprised."

I thought about that as I threw Latte's ball again. Why hadn't Dean mentioned this Sean guy if he seemed like such an obvious suspect to Karen? Did he think Alex was a more plausible suspect to blame it on? Or was Dean actually innocent and genuinely thought Alex killed Georgina? I needed to track Sean Donnelly down and talk to him. I was pretty sure it was too late to catch him at the high school. "Do you know where Sean lives?"

She looked at me out of the corner of her eye. I hadn't told her I was investigating Georgina's death, and it probably sounded strange that I wanted to know the address of the person she thought killed her coworker. Not that I expected her to know it. I didn't know the home address of anyone who came in to my café unless I was friends with them.

"Over on Surfside Drive," she said, surprising me. "I don't know the house number, but it's a little white house with green shutters."

Now I looked at her out of the corner of my eye. Before I could say anything, she answered my unspoken question. "My friend lives down the street. I've seen him come and go."

"Are you sure that's his house?"

"Yeah, I asked her since I knew who he was, and I was curious."

At least I had a sister in curiosity. I threw Latte's ball. "Do you know his girlfriend's name?"

She made a little bit of a face. "Celine? Fantine? Delphine? Something Frenchy with an 'een' at the end, I think. I don't know. I'm not great with names." She smiled. "Francesca."

"You can call me Fran."

"Yeah, I'm not going to remember that."

"Do you mind if I ask you a couple more questions?" I realized I was starting to sound like a weirdo with my borderline interrogation.

She gave me the side-eye again.

"I'm kind of helping out with the investigation," I said before remembering Mike's warning that I absolutely was not officially involved and shouldn't do or say anything that might suggest that. "I mean, I'm not working for the police or anything. I'm just looking into it on my own. For Georgina. She deserves to have her killer found."

Still the side-eye. This time, I decided to wait. I threw Latte's tennis ball.

Finally, after the setter had returned and dropped his slobbery ball in Karen's hand, she answered me. "Yeah, ask me whatever you want if you think it'll help catch the guy who did this. A brick to the head is a crappy way to go."

"Had you heard anything about Dean and Georgina arguing lately?"

"You mean more than usual?"

"Fighting was a normal thing with them?"

"Yeah, you know." She shrugged. "They bickered. He didn't like the way she'd set up a display and say something, and she'd get kind of snippy back. Nothing major. Not like the way she fought with Alex. I actually kind of wondered if there was something going on between them—it was that kind of fighting."

There was so much there I didn't know what to start with. I decided to start at the end. "You thought there might be something going on between Georgina and Dean?"

She shrugged again. It seemed to be her default move. "I dunno. I mean, I don't think they were actually hooking up or anything, but the tension was through the roof."

"Sexual tension?"

"Yup." She chucked the tennis ball. "That's how I interpreted it anyway."

Well, that was some new information. "Had they been fighting any more than usual lately?"

Karen thought for a minute. "Maybe a little. The past couple months or so. Not a lot, but, yeah, I think it was more. I mostly tried to tune it out."

"You said she used to fight with Alex?" I asked even though I'd already heard about it from Sammy. I wanted to hear someone else's perspective.

"Oh, my God, yes! For months after they broke up. He'd come by the shop, and they'd get in screaming matches."

"In the store?"

"No, they'd go out back, but you could still hear them."

"Do you know what they fought about?"

"Really stupid stuff. 'Your crap's still at my house.' 'If you weren't out partying every night, maybe I could come and get it.' 'You're always nagging me.' 'You never listen to anything I say.' Blah, blah, blah. *Drama*. I tried to ignore that too."

For someone who said she tried to ignore her coworker's fighting, she sure knew a lot about it. "Was he still coming around?"

She thought briefly as she threw her dog's ball. "No, I guess he finally gave up."

"On Georgina picking up her stuff?"

"No, on them getting back together. That's what I think he really wanted, even if he couldn't stop acting like a jerk long enough for Georgina to stop being mad at him."

Dean had mentioned that Alex couldn't stand Georgina not being with him, so Karen wasn't the only one who thought that. "Did Alex ever get... violent?"

Karen's reaction was immediate. She shook her head vigorously. "No. Uh-uh. I mean, he'd yell, but I never even saw him slam his hand down on a table or anything."

"So you don't think he would have hurt her?" I felt like I was grilling her with all my questions.

"No, and I mean, like I said, a brick's a crappy murder weapon."

"Maybe he just threw it through the window to scare her and got really unlucky?"

She rolled her eyes at me. "So he decided to very specifically steal the most expensive thing in the store too? Just for the heck of it? Sure."

Maybe not. Her point about a brick being a poor choice of a murder weapon made sense. I started to think that the police might have been on the right track with the robbery angle. I wondered if they knew about Sean the Janitor. I threw Latte's ball. "Have the police talked to you?"

"Yup. Yesterday."

Of course they had. Like Mike had said, it wasn't his first day on the job. "Did you tell them about Sean?"

"Sure did."

"Did they seem like they believed you?"

She shrugged. "I dunno. That guy's hard to read. Really good looking but hard to read." She bounced her dog's ball in her hand. "You don't know if he's married, do you?" The setter took off as she threw the ball.

I glanced at the naked third finger of her left hand. Apparently, she was in the market. "Which one was it?" There were only a couple of possibilities.

"Bad with names, remember?" She cocked her thumb toward her chest. "Tall. Dark hair. Handsome. You know him?"

"Suit?"

"Yup," she said, a little dreamily. A slight smile played at her lips. I felt a little weird about her making that face over him.

"Mike Stanton. Married. Happily. Two kids. He's very devoted to them."

She sighed. "Oh, well."

Latte, who had been slowing down over his last few fetches, dropped his ball at my feet instead of in my hand and lay down in the grass.

"Looks like somebody's tired," Karen said.

"Yeah. Yours is still going pretty strong, though."

"I don't think he ever gets tired."

"Irish setter, right? They have a lot of energy, don't they?"

"Yup. And yours is a..." She squinted at Latte on the ground. I waited for her to declare him a mutt. "Berger Picard?"

I was so shocked I stumbled back a little. "How did you know?" No one except the veterinarian had ever recognized Latte's breed. On top of being incredibly rare, Picards are so shaggy and generic looking that they don't seem like they could be purebreds. They look like some kind of mutt.

"I used to work on movies out in LA. We liked to use Picards because they don't look like anything special, but they look the same, so you could swap them out if you needed to."

I stared at her in surprise. Karen used to work in Hollywood? I had no idea. Maybe that explained her oddly ageless appearance. Looking at her more closely, I thought I could see some evidence of a few nips and tucks on her face. I'd seen enough nose jobs in New York to be practically an expert at spotting them. "What are you doing back here?"

"Long story." She smirked. "What's his name?" She nodded back at Latte, still sprawled on the ground at my feet. Her dog walked over and looked at him then went back to Karen and waited for her to throw his ball again.

"Latte," I said as Karen threw the ball across the lawn. Latte lifted his head and looked at me to find out why I was saying his name. After a few seconds, he gave up and dropped his head back down. "Yours?"

"Red."

Apparently, both of us got the inspiration for our dogs' names from their colors since Red was red, and Latte was exactly the color of a perfectly poured latte.

"How old is he?" she asked. "He, right?"

"Yup, he's a he. The vet said he thinks he's about three. He was a stray, so we're not really sure."

"A stray Picard? That's unusual. Most people don't give them up once they get their hands on one."

"Yeah, that's kind of a long story too." I glanced down at Latte, who looked more than ready to get going. I was ready to go see if I could track down Sean the Janitor too. "Well," I said, "I guess I'd better get going if I'm going to get anything done today. The café doesn't run itself after all."

"Murders don't solve themselves, you mean."

"That too." I smiled at her. "It was nice to meet you. Formally, anyway."

I leaned down and hooked Latte's leash back onto his collar. I think we both breathed a sigh of relief that we were safely back on the right side of the law. Either that or I sighed with relief, and he just panted.

"Yup, you too. Lemme know if you have any other questions."

"Thanks. Um, how can I get in touch with you?" I started digging in my pocket for my phone so I could save her number in it.

"I'm here most days, about this time. And I guess I'll probably be working some extra hours at the jewelry shop whenever that reopens."

"Okay." I pulled my hand back out of my pocket. It seemed Karen wasn't interested in being all that available. "Well, I'll see you around."

I waited for her to say something back, but all I got was a slight wave of her hand that could have just been her swatting a bug.

I headed out of the park in the direction of Surfside Drive and the little white house with green shutters where Sean the Janitor was supposed to live.

Chapter Twelve

The houses along Surfside Drive were probably about the same age as the ones on my street—it seemed like everything in Cape Bay was either built in the Colonial or postwar era—but they were much more worn looking. Surfside was closer to the beach and had fewer trees dotting the landscape to protect its houses from the elements, leaving their wood and paint vulnerable to the brutal effects of salt and sand.

The little white house with green shutters that Karen had directed me toward was about halfway down the street. The white paint on the siding was peeling, and the green on the shutters had faded from what

I guessed used to be a dark forest color to more of a grayish green, still green enough to be green, but not really a color you'd actually want to paint your house.

The grass in the yard managed to be overgrown even though it was October. Matt had given up mowing my yard—he's such a good boyfriend—in early September, so I figured Sean the Janitor must have stopped sometime back in August before school started. I guessed it was the same principle as the joke about a mechanic's car always being broken. The janitor's house was run down because he was too busy keeping up the school to take care of his own house.

The garden, however, was immaculate. There were asters, chrysanthemums, and other flowers I didn't know the names of but that I was used to seeing in my green-thumbed neighbors' gardens. They were mostly orange and yellow with a sprinkling of red and pink. Around the edge was a neat stone border. It had an almost casual, haphazard look to it, but when I looked closely, I saw that it was a little too perfectly arranged. It made the place look homey despite the less-maintained bits around it. Unless Sean the Janitor was a passionate gardener who couldn't be brought to mow once in a while, I suspected it was the work of his girlfriend with the Frenchy name that ended in –een.

I pushed open the gate of the white picket fence and headed up the short front walk, laid with decorative bricks. I wondered if the same person who had done the garden border had done the front walk and how much they charged. Redoing the path from the sidewalk up to my house would be a nice way of putting my own stamp on the place.

Latte followed politely at my side as I made my way toward the front door. He seemed interested in exploring the yard, but I kept the leash wrapped around my hand so he couldn't wander too far away from me.

I leaned toward the door as I pushed the doorbell to see if I could hear it ring inside. The little light was out on it, and I wasn't sure if that meant the whole thing wasn't working. I didn't hear anything inside, but I wasn't necessarily sure if that meant anything either. I waited a couple of seconds until I was sure I didn't hear any movement in the house then rapped on the door. I stood back a little and rocked on my toes while I waited for someone to open the door.

After a minute or so, I knocked again, harder this time. Almost immediately, the door swung open, and I blurted out the Frenchy name that ended in –een.

"Sabine!"

She gave me a look that was half scowl and half surprise. "You're the lady from the coffee shop, right? Did I forget something or something?" She looked down at Latte and screwed up her face even more.

"No, no, you didn't forget anything. And yes, I'm from the coffee shop, but that's not why I'm here."

She looked at my skeptically, and I plowed ahead.

"I'm looking for Sean, actually. Is he home?"

Sabine stepped back and put one hand on her hip. "Whaddaya wanna see Sean for?" Her Massachusetts accent came out in full force. It was the tone tough girls used to use in high school when they were ready to start punching somebody. Even though I'd been taking kickboxing classes at the local gym, I wasn't eager to test my skills in a fight with Sabine.

I took a step back while I scrambled to come up with a good excuse for why I was looking for Sean. I didn't think Sabine would be too fond of hearing that I wanted to ask Sean if he'd killed Georgina. "Oh, um, it's business, actually."

She raised one eyebrow and flexed the hand that wasn't on her hip.

"Did you hear about the jewelry store down on Main Street that got broken into? Where the girl got killed? Howard Jewelers?" I asked, realizing I wasn't going to get away with being too vague. I saw her tough guy act falter the tiniest bit and thought I might be on the right track. "The owner, Dean, is a friend of mine." Not a total lie. "And since he's busy with the police and the insurance company and stuff, he asked me to follow up with some customers, let them know the status of their orders, the reopening schedule, stuff like that."

"Sean was a customer?"

I shrugged and tried to look nonchalant. "He was on Dean's list. I guess he had his address but not his phone number for some reason."

"What was he buying there?"

I saw an opportunity. I hadn't planned on talking to Sean's girlfriend, but if he was the murderer, she might be able to give me some useful information. "I think Dean said it was a—" I paused and put a thoughtful look on my face then gasped like I'd just remembered. I looked at her closely. "I'm not sure if I should tell you."

"Why not?"

"Are you his girlfriend?" I let my slight Massachusetts accent thicken. It wasn't as strong as hers, but it was enough to give away that I had grown up in the Bay State.

"Yeah, why?"

"Oh, well, just that—" I looked at her again with the expression I hoped looked thoughtful. "I think it may be a gift. For you. I don't want to ruin the surprise if it is."

"Oh, no, I know all about it," she spat out without hesitation. She was a better liar than I was.

"You do? About the engagement—" I cut myself off and tried to look horrified that I'd let the secret slip. I covered my mouth with the hand that wasn't wrapped up in Latte's leash.

"Engagement ring?" she gasped, looking actually surprised. Maybe she wasn't such a great liar after all. I wished I knew some of those fancy police techniques for detecting lies. I tried to subtly look for beads of perspiration breaking out on her forehead. "Uh, yeah, I know about it. I mean, I didn't realize Sean had already bought it or anything. I thought he was still, uh, thinking about it."

"I'm not sure about all the details. I just know that Dean wanted me to let Sean know that there was a problem with the purchase."

"What kind of problem?"

"Don't know. Dean didn't say." I glanced around then leaned closer as if I was going to let her in on a secret. "I don't know this for sure, but I think it was probably stolen in the robbery." I leaned back and shrugged like it was no big deal. "At least it shouldn't be hard for you guys to pick a new one, right? I mean, a ring is a ring, isn't it?" I watched Sabine closely for her reaction. She was definitely breathing harder than she had been. She swallowed hard.

"No, not this one."

I made a face like I didn't understand. "What do you mean?"

"The ring Sean was getting me was special. It was a real gorgeous ring. It had all these diamonds." She waved her right hand in a general circle over her left hand. "It was so nice. An antique."

"Ohhh," I said as if I was suddenly understanding. "You can't really replace an antique, can you?"

"No." She was clearly upset, but I couldn't tell if she looked more like she wanted to scream or cry. Whichever it was, I definitely had her convinced that Sean had worked out a way to buy her that ring. And now, since "Dean" had wanted to make sure that Sean knew there was a problem with the ring, if Sean tried to give it to Sabine, she'd know that he hadn't bought it for her after all. He'd stolen it and killed a woman in the process. Unless, of course, she already knew that and was playing dumb to try to protect him.

"So, um, is Sean here?" I asked after a few seconds of watching her and trying to figure out where she was on her emotional roller coaster.

"No, he's at football practice."

"Sean plays football?"

"Not anymore. He did back in high school though. He was the quarterback." She sounded exceptionally proud of Sean's high school football prowess. "He coaches now, over at the high school. The kids like him 'cause he's not an old fogey like some of the other coaches."

"How long will he be there?"

She looked at me with an eyebrow raised and her lip curled. "Why?"

"Because I need to tell him about the ring." Didn't I just explain that to her?

"You just told me. I can tell him."

Time for some more quick thinking. "Oh, I'm sure you would. And I would let you, except Dean, well, he can be kind of a stickler for things. If he asks—and he will—if I talked to Sean, and I say I talked to you instead, he'd have a fit, especially since it's about an engagement ring." I rolled my eyes dramatically to make it seem like I thought the mandates I'd made up on Dean's behalf were ridiculous.

"So lie."

"Oh, I'm a terrible liar. He'd see right through me."

She stared at me for an uncomfortably long time then exhaled sharply with her own roll of the eyes. "He'll be at the school until five or six, then he usually goes over to the Sand Bar for a drink with the guys."

"Okay, great, thanks!" I took a step backward to make my escape then paused. "By the way, I was wondering, who did all the stonework out here? It's beautiful."

Sabine made another one of her faces. She looked uncomfortable for a second, and for some reason, I wondered if she didn't want to tell me because she didn't want anyone else to have stonework that rivaled hers. Either that or she was confused by my sudden compliment in light of her fairly unpleasant treatment of me, which probably made more sense.

"I dunno. It was here when I moved in."

It looked fairly new, so I wondered if she was telling the truth. Karen hadn't said anything to indicate that Sean and Sabine had only recently moved into the little white and green house, but she hadn't said that they'd lived there for years either, so maybe it didn't matter.

I turned to leave again then stopped. "One last thing. Do you know where Sean was Monday night? Around ten?"

"What, are you the cops or something?" Sabine took a slightly threatening step toward me. I backed away even farther.

"No." I shook my head quickly. I still wanted to avoid that punch down. "I'm just asking. Since I'm friends with Dean and all."

"He was home all night. With me," she said angrily before stepping back inside and slamming the door.

I felt I'd hit a nerve. I didn't think Sean had been home with Sabine all night Monday at all.

I waited until I was off Surfside Drive to pull my phone out of my pocket. As much as I wanted to go straight to the high school to talk to Sean, Latte was starting to drag beside me, worn out first from the long game of fetch and then from our walk across town from the park. I had to take him home. I tapped at the screen of my phone to pull up the number I wanted and then hit the green call button.

"Antonia's Italian Café, this is Rhonda. How may I help you?"

"Hey, it's Fran."

"Fran! How's it going? You catch a murderer yet?"

I chuckled a little. "Nope, you?"

"No, but Mike's already been back for another cup of coffee. I don't know how that man sleeps at night with as much as he drinks. I don't think we're his only supplier either."

"I'm pretty sure he gets some down at the station too."

"I've had the stuff they call coffee down there. I'm not sure the term applies."

"When have you had the coffee at the police station?" I suddenly wondered if the woman I'd left in charge of my café had been keeping some rather significant secrets from me.

"I'd love to say I was there for something interesting, but my older boy did an internship last summer that required him to be fingerprinted, and the police department is the place to do it."

"Sounds like fun."

"Oh, it was. But anyway, what's up? You calling to check in? You don't think I'm capable of taking care of the place on my own?"

"Actually, I wanted to see if you'd be okay with me staying out a little bit longer. I was hoping to talk to someone else before I came back."

"No problem. Becky got here a little while ago, and between the two of us, we're keeping the Bay well caffeinated."

"Things aren't too busy?"

"Stop it! No. Everything's fine. We're a well-oiled machine."

"Okay, good. Thanks. I shouldn't be too long."

"Take your time. Like I said, we're fine here."

We said goodbye, and I disconnected the call. I looked at the time on my phone. Latte and I were only about halfway home, and I still had to walk back to the high school. I had a car sitting in my driveway, but Cape Bay was so small, I pretty much walked everywhere. Between growing up in the little seaside town and living for years in New York City, cars to me were only necessary when you were going a long way or carrying a lot of things. The mile or so from my house to the high school was not a long way, and I had nothing to carry, so I'd walk.

I pulled up Matt's number on my phone. I hadn't talked to him all day, and even though I would have been too embarrassed to admit it, I missed him. The phone rang enough times that when it finally picked up, I was startled to hear Matt in person instead of his voice mail

"Matt Cardosi."

"Is it a bad time?"

"Hey, Franny!" I heard the smile in his voice, and it made my heart flutter a little in my chest. "No, it's a great time. I'm just getting back to my desk after a meeting. What's up?"

"Nothing. Latte and I were just out for a walk, and I thought I'd call and say hi."

"Uh-huh, how's the investigation going? Who'd you leave in charge at the café?"

"What makes you think I'm investigating?"

I heard his chuckle. "The sun is up."

"I'm not that bad!"

"No, you're not. But usually, when you walk Latte during the day, it's a quick trip around the block, not anything you take the time to call me during."

"Maybe I'm turning over a new leaf."

"Or maybe you're walking across town to ask someone some questions and figured you had time to call me."

"I'm actually walking Latte back home. Thank you very much," I said with more indignation in my voice than I actually felt.

"Oh, so you're done questioning somebody. Find out anything new?"

"Yeah, I think I actually have a good lead."

"Someone other than Dean or Alex?"

"Yup, a guy called Sean Donnelly. Do you know him?"

I heard Matt muttering Sean's name on his end of the line. "Sounds kind of familiar, but I can't really place him. He lives in Cape Bay?"

"Yeah. He's one of the coaches on the football team. Apparently, he played quarterback in high school."

"Ah, now I know who you're talking about. You think he killed Georgina?"

"I don't know yet. I need to talk to him before I make up my mind. Oh, Matty? Quarterbacks—are they throwing football guys or running football guys? Or are those the same?"

There was a long silence on the other end of the line.

"Matty?"

"Yes," Matt said quietly.

"Are you okay?"

"Yeah, I just—I'm trying to figure whether it's worse that my girlfriend doesn't know what the quarterback does or that she calls them 'football guys.'"

"Well, what am I supposed to call them?"

"Football players, Franny. They're football players."

"Okay, *football players*. But what about the quarterback? Does he throw or run?"

Matt sighed heavily. "He throws. Why are you asking?"

"I'm just wondering if a guy who used to be a quarterback would have good brick-throwing skills."

"I don't think it takes much skill to throw a brick through a plate-glass window, Franny."

"No? You don't think so?"

"You're just messing with me, aren't you?"

"Pretty much. I really wasn't sure what the quarterback does though."

"You could watch the Patriots with me on Sunday, and I could explain it all to you."

"That sounds incredibly boring."

Matt laughed out loud, and I wondered what his coworkers thought. "At least you're honest."

"It's the least I can do. Hey, dinner tonight?"

"You want to go out?"

"Yeah, that might be good."

"Okay, sounds good. Listen, I hate to cut you off, but I have a conference call in a few minutes I have to get ready for."

"No problem. I'll see you tonight."

"Okay."

There was the awkward pause.

"Um, bye."

"Bye, Franny."

I sighed as I slid my phone back into my pocket. One of these days, one of us was going to have to break down and be the first to say, "I love you," but it didn't look like today was going to be that day.

Chapter Thirteen

It didn't take all that long to get home to drop Latte off at the house. As soon as I opened the door, he ran straight to his bowl and spent a while lapping up the water then went up the stairs without even casting a second glance at me. Based on previous experience, it was safe to assume that when I got home later that evening, I'd find him sprawled out in his favorite spot on my bed, passed out and drooling without a worry in the world.

"Okay, bye!" I called even though I knew he couldn't care less.

The walk over to the high school didn't take long. Even though it had been fifteen years, I felt like I could practically walk there in my sleep. I smiled, remembering how

Matt and I had walked to school together every day for four years. We'd been close friends growing up, but only that. We flirted a lot, but there was never anything between us until I came back to Cape Bay after my mother's death. I wondered if I'd missed out on almost twenty years of a good thing by not getting together with him sooner. I certainly would have saved myself some of the heartbreaks I'd acquired over the years if I'd been with him.

I sighed, thinking about what things might have been like if we'd gotten together in high school. We might have gotten married after college, bought a house of our own, had some babies. I probably never would have spent ten years working in public relations for high-profile clients. Would I have become the same person I was if I hadn't had those experiences? I decided it was better not to spend too much time thinking about what might have been when what I had right now was perfect. Who knows? I might not have ended up with Matt at all.

My arrival at the high school snapped me out of my reverie. It still resembled the school I'd gone to, but there had been so much remodeling and new construction, it was hard to see the old building in there. I wondered if the football field was still in the same place. Only one way to find out.

I headed around the back of the school. Yup, there it was, right behind the building. I remembered sitting in my senior English class and looking out the window as a big machine aerated the field. I also remembered sitting on the bleachers after the school was evacuated because somebody called in a bomb threat, wondering if we'd really be safe there if the school exploded. Even as an adult, I was pretty sure we wouldn't have been.

The football team was out on the field, running back and forth, tapping their hands on the ground each time they turned. *It would probably actually make a good fitness class.* If boot camp classes were so popular, why not a football camp class? *Maybe I should mention it at the gym.* And then as the players started running up the bleachers, I questioned why I would even want to suggest new ways for them to torture us. Perhaps football camp was an idea best kept to myself.

I walked over to the first person I saw, a boy who looked about twelve years old, but who I figured was probably a high school student. I didn't remember the boys looking so small and young when I was in school. I'd have to get my old yearbooks out to see if Matt and Mike looked like little babies when we were that age.

"Excuse me." The boy looked up. "I'm looking for Sean Donnelly?"

He pointed wordlessly across the field and took a slug from his water bottle.

"Thank you."

He grunted.

I headed across the field to where the man he had indicated was talking to another one of the players. He held a football in his hand and made throwing motions. *Throwing.* I knew Matt had said that it wasn't exactly hard to throw a brick through a window, and part of me agreed with him, but another part of me felt like it was still a bit of evidence. Sean Donnelly had experience with throwing things long distances and accurately. Of course, he'd hit Georgina in the head when he probably—I hoped—hadn't intended to, but still. It was circumstantial evidence at best.

They didn't even look in my direction as I approached. I waited a minute or so to see if they would acknowledge me, but apparently, I was rendered invisible by the siren's call of the football. "Sean?" I asked finally.

They looked up.

"I'm looking for Sean Donnelly." I looked at the older of the two. "Is that you?"

"Who's asking?"

"Um, me?" Wow, this guy and Sabine made a pair with their attitudes. There was a term for Massachusites who acted like that, but after the time my grandmother had laid into me after hearing me say it, I'd never been able to bring myself to let it pass my lips again. Of course, my grandfather had laughed uproariously at his nine-year-old granddaughter calling a particularly unpleasant customer that, but I'd still kept it out of my vocabulary.

"And who are you?" the man asked.

I decided to stick to the same story I'd given Sabine, just in case they compared notes. "I'm Francesca Amaro. I'm friends with Dean Howard from the jewelry store. I'm assuming you heard about the robbery?"

"The one where the girl died?" the boy asked.

"Yes, that one." I smiled at him, though it felt like a weird subject to smile over. Still, he might be a useful ally.

"Get out of here, Lawson." The man waved his hand at the boy. The boy took off jogging across the field, helmet dangling from his hand. It crossed my mind that it might not have been wise to approach a man who might be a murderer all on my own. "What do you want?"

"Are you Sean?"

"Yeah, who else would I be?"

I don't know, any other coach on the team? I kept that to myself. "Just making sure." I plastered what I hoped was a pleasant smile on my face. He didn't seem impressed. "Anyway, Dean asked me to get in touch with some of his customers—"

"I'm not a customer," Sean interrupted.

"No? You were in the notes Dean gave me as having been in recently about an engagement ring." I wished I'd brought a notebook along so I could pretend to refer to it.

"Yeah, I can't afford that thing."

"Oh, Dean said you'd been negotiating."

"That guy doesn't negotiate. He strong arms. He wouldn't let me work out a payment plan on it or anything."

"Hmm, I guess maybe the notes he gave me were a little out of date."

Sean didn't respond. I needed to push harder.

"So you weren't still in the market for a ring?"

"I was in the market for a ring, just not that one."

"Because you didn't want it anymore or—"

"Because I couldn't afford it, lady! Don't you listen?"

"Sorry." I forced a laugh. "I—the notes—" I needed to find a different approach. "Just so I can make sure I have it right when I tell Dean, you are not interested in the ring at all anymore?"

"I was never interested in it. My girlfriend was. It's kind of hard to be interested in something that costs more than I get paid in a year."

I forced another laugh. "I get it. So I guess what I'm asking—again, just so I don't mess it up when I tell Dean—you weren't still looking for ways to get it for your girlfriend?"

"No, lady, I wasn't. I knew I was never going to be able to get it for her. She's the one who made me keep going in there to ask if I could get a discount. She's the one who couldn't get her mind off of it. I was done thinking about that. If she doesn't want to marry me because I couldn't buy her the most expensive ring in the state, that's her problem, not mine. I got no problem staying single."

I wasn't sure if I should ask my next question, but I did it anyway. What was the worst that could happen? He probably wouldn't haul off and kill me with a football to the head—if that was even possible. "So you wouldn't steal it for her?"

Sean stared at me for a minute, not saying anything. "What'd you say, lady? Are you accusing me of something? You think I killed that girl?"

"No, no, not at all. I'm only asking questions. Dean's a little worked up about the robbery and the girl dying and all. He's going to ask me if I asked you, and I'm a terrible liar, so he'd know if I didn't but said I did." When all else fails, blame someone else.

"A'right, well, whatever. I can't stand around talking to you all day. I got a football practice to get back to."

"Okay, no problem. Thanks for talking to me," I said as he started across the field toward everyone else. "Um, one last thing!"

He turned around and faced me, looking pretty disgusted.

"Where were you Monday night?"

Now he looked really disgusted. I thought he was going to swear at me, but he didn't. "I was at home with Sabine. Now get lost."

After that conversation, I was more than happy to oblige.

Chapter Fourteen

I picked up burgers and fried oysters from Sandy's Seafood Shack on my way home after closing up the café. If I was going to buy him dinner, I had to be sneaky about it.

"I brought dinner!" I called as I walked into my house.

Matt sat on the couch with Latte, watching ESPN. "I thought we were going out!"

"I lied." I dropped the paper bag off on the coffee table. The grease from the oysters had already made significant progress soaking through the bag. "Has Latte eaten?"

"According to me or him?"

"You." I laughed. I didn't have to ask to know what Latte's opinion would be.

"Yeah, he ate."

I grabbed some paper plates, a bottle of red wine, a corkscrew, and two glasses and carried them into the living room.

"Classy." Matt eyed what I had in my hands.

"I didn't have any disposable cups. Hey, don't feed him that!"

Latte snatched the fried oyster off of Matt's outstretched hand. "It's okay for him to have one," Matt said. "I looked it up."

"It's fried. It'll make him sick." I plopped down on the couch next to Matt.

"That's okay. I'll clean it up." He leaned around me, and I thought he was going to grab the bottle and corkscrew since we'd established that that was his job, but instead, he put his hand on the side of my face and kissed me so long and soft I almost forgot about dinner. Just before I did though, his hand dropped from my cheek down to the bottle and corkscrew. "Okay, let's eat!"

I stared at him, my mind too muddled to think of any response that would be considered remotely clever or romantic, until he winked at me. Then I giggled. He popped the bottle open and filled our two glasses, far beyond the point that wine experts say you're supposed to. He took a paper plate for himself and handed one to me before digging in the greasy bag for our burgers.

"Sorry, boy," he said as Latte eyed the fried oyster Matt was popping into his own mouth. "Mom said no."

"Don't pit my dog against me!"

"He already knows you're no fun."

I swatted at him. He grinned and ate another oyster.

We were almost done eating and what seemed like an eternity into some show where two men yelled at each other about draft picks when Matt nudged me. "So how'd it go today?"

"At the café? Fine."

He gave me a look. "Your investigation."

"I don't know."

"You don't know?"

"Well, I talked to it seemed like everybody today. Dean, Mike, Sabine, Sean–"

"Sabine?"

"Sean's girlfriend."

"And Mike?"

"Stanton? You know, the detective? We grew up with him?" I wondered if he really didn't know who I meant.

"Yeah, I know who Mike is. I was asking what you talked to him about."

"He gave me a lecture. I'll tell you about it later."

"Okay, go on."

"So I talked to a bunch of people today, and I learned a lot, but I don't really know if I'm any closer to knowing who did it than I was this morning." I slouched down in the couch, turning the day's events over in my mind.

"Really? You didn't get any useful information?"

"No, I got a lot of useful information. I just don't know who it points to."

"I see." He ate the last fried oyster.

"I mean, Dean still seems... I don't know, *off* somehow. There's something wrong with what he's saying and how he's acting, but I can't tell if he's lying to me or just hiding something."

"Aren't those kind of the same? Lie of commission versus lie of omission?"

"Yeah, I guess." I sighed.

"So you think he did it?"

"I don't know."

"What's your gut telling you?" He poked me in the stomach.

I squirmed away from him. "That dinner was really greasy."

He laughed and pulled me back over to him. "What else? You talked to that Sean guy, right? What did you think of him?"

"I'm not interested in socializing with him and his girlfriend anytime soon. That's for sure."

"So they're nice people?"

I scoffed. "They do the state proud."

Matt laughed. He knew what I meant.

"They're both really abrasive. He doesn't actually seem like he cares if they ever get married. They live together, so I think it's kind of a why-buy-the-cow situation for him."

"I'm sorry, a what?" Matt sounded utterly baffled. "Where did cows come from? Is that another word for an engagement ring?"

I laughed. "You've never heard that? 'Why buy the cow when you can get the milk for free?'"

Matt shook his head, still looking confused.

"It's what people say about not living together before you get married. Why would a guy marry you when you're already living there?"

"Hold on. Are you the cow in this scenario?"

I laughed as I nodded. I'd heard the saying so many times growing up that I'd never stopped to think about how bizarre it would sound if you were hearing it for the first time.

"Wow, and I'm the—?"

"The farmer?" I suggested, still laughing.

"And where did you hear this? Is this a New York thing?"

I cracked up. "No! It's a—I don't know. It's just a thing. My mom and my grandmother used to say it to me all the time growing up. A behave-yourself-if-you-want to-ev-er-get-married kind of thing. I guess nobody says it to boys?"

"Wow." Matt leaned back on the couch. "That does not speak highly of men."

"I thought it was bad enough that it was calling women cows, but I guess you're right. It doesn't really make men look good either."

"Just wow." Matt shook his head.

"Anyway, it really didn't seem like Sean cared that much about marrying Sabine."

"So that lead didn't really pan out, huh?"

"Nope."

"What else do you have?"

"I think that's about it. I want to go track Alex down tomorrow, but..." I flopped my hands in the air.

"But what?"

"I don't know. That's it. That's all I have. I'm going to go talk to Alex tomorrow, and Dean seems like he's hiding something. That's it." I looked up at the clock. Five to ten. "It's been forty-eight hours, and I have nothing. Supposedly, if there's not a suspect in the first forty-eight hours, the case is unlikely to be solved." I crossed my arms across my chest. I was pouting a little, but I was frustrated.

"Franny." Matt tucked his hand under my chin and tipped it up toward him.

"What?"

"This is, what, the fourth murder we've had?"

I nodded.

"And you've investigated them all."

I nodded again.

"In any one of those, did you figure out who did it within the first forty-eight hours?"

I shook my head.

"So why should this time be any different?"

I shrugged.

"Because you know about the forty-eight-hour thing now?"

"Maybe."

"Besides, I think that's for cops. You're not a cop."

"You sound like Mike."

"Was that the lecture you got today?"

"More or less."

"You know he just wants to make sure you're not getting in over your head."

"He wants to make sure I'm not screwing up his case."

"Whatever. It's nothing personal."

I grunted. "I'm not so sure about that."

"No, he likes you. He wouldn't let you get away with so much if he didn't."

"If you say so."

"I say so."

"Can we watch something else? I don't even understand what they're talking about." I was done talking about the case. I wanted to think about something else, and whatever the angry bald men were arguing about wasn't doing it for me.

"Franchise tags," Matt non-explained.

I stared at him blankly.

"The Nineteen Eighty-Two World Series is on ESPN Classic."

"Was that the one where the ball rolled through the guy's legs?" It was the only World Series moment I knew of.

"No, that was eighty-six."

"I wouldn't want to watch that anyway."

Matt chuckled and hit the Guide button on the remote then tossed it to me. I found a movie I'd watched at least twenty times and put it on.

"This is really what you want to watch? Isn't this the one you can put on mute and still quote all the dialog?"

"Yes and yes." I snuggled into him. I could smell the warm, spicy fragrance of his cologne when I was this close.

"Then let's watch it," he said, even though I knew he wasn't really excited about it.

I tipped my head up to look at him. I didn't know how I hadn't seen growing up how handsome he was with his dark brown eyes, his thick dark hair that was getting just a little long, and the five o'clock shadow dusting his cheeks. He glanced down at me and smiled. I almost told him I loved him, but instead, I bit my lip and turned back to the movie.

Chapter Fifteen

The next day, I had plans to meet with my whole staff at the café in the afternoon to go over the plan for while I was in Italy. It was mostly basic stuff—making sure everyone knew when they were scheduled to work, going over everything to do at open and close, confirming all the daily procedures, including who was covering each of the tasks I usually did.

I'd arranged for Monica to bring extras of her desserts in case we ran out. Sammy and Rhonda had the recipes for the ones I usually made and the numbers for the people we bought the rest of them from. I'd gone ahead and placed a larger-than-usual supply order to make sure they didn't run out of napkins while I was gone, and we'd already gone over how the orders were placed in case they needed anything else. I knew I was leaving Antonia's in capable hands, but the fact that I couldn't think of the last time a member of the Amaro family hadn't been there to take care of things made me a little bit nervous.

But that was in the afternoon. My morning was wide open. My talk with Matt the night before had encouraged me about my investigation into Georgina's murder, and I felt confident about tracking down Alex to talk to him about Georgina. I'd found out the name of Alex's company from Sammy and where it was in town. I'd also gotten from her the address where he and Georgina had lived together. Alex actually still lived there, but I would talk to him at his office. I wanted the address to talk to the neighbors about Alex and Georgina's fighting.

I went ahead and put on my work clothes since I was planning to visit Alex's office last, and it was just down the street from the café. I pulled a black long sleeve T-shirt on over my head and paired it with black jeans. My mother's sensible-but-stylish black Italian leather loafers went on my feet. I briefly considered leaving my hair down for the day, but as soon as I thought about standing over the steaming espresso machine with my thick mop of black hair hanging down around my shoulders, I pulled it up into a high ponytail.

Once I got Latte all squared away for the morning, I headed out in the direction of Alex's neighborhood. It was farther inland than mine by about a half mile. It was always remarkable to me how you could go such a short distance away and have the smell of the ocean be so much harder to detect. I was glad I could open the windows in my house and let the tangy, salty smell in. It smelled like Cape Bay, and I wouldn't feel at home without it.

Alex's house was about halfway down his street. It was simple, modest, and much newer than mine, a generic ranch with no real style, but the lawn was mowed, and there were a few bushes in the garden that looked like they had recently been trimmed. It looked as if he at least put some effort into taking care of it. I didn't knock on his door.

Instead, I went next door. The woman who answered looked like she was about fifty. Her hair was graying, but her makeup was neatly done and her T-shirt and jeans looked new, or at least well taken care of. I didn't recognize her, but there were a lot of people I didn't recognize in Cape Bay since I came back to town. She had a pleasant enough look on her face, which I took as a good sign.

"Hi! My name is Francesca Amaro and—"

"Sorry, I'm not interested." She started closing the door.

"I'm sorry?"

"I'm not interested. Whatever you're selling, I'm not interested." She pushed the door farther closed.

"No, no, I'm not selling anything!"

She paused her closing, but looked at me warily.

"I'm—I wanted to ask you about Alex and Georgina, your neighbors."

"Georgina doesn't live there anymore." She got the door almost closed before I put my hand out to stop it.

"I know. She's dead. I'm trying to help figure out who killed her!"

The woman let up her pressure on the door a little bit. "You're with the police?"

"No. I was a friend of hers. Her boss, Dean, the store owner, asked me if I would see if I could find out anything about who might have killed her."

"Why are you asking about her and Alex?" She seemed to warm up to me a little.

"I understand they fought a lot?"

"I thought you said you were her friend. Her friends would know if she and Alex fought."

I was losing her. I was going to have to stretch the truth a little. "I know they fought. But you know how people are. What she said happened and what other people saw aren't necessarily the same thing."

"Well, you're right about that, but I don't see what that has to do with her getting killed like that. It was a robbery, wasn't it? Unless—unless you think it wasn't. Unless you think Alex had something to do with it. Are you saying you think Alex killed her?"

"Do you think he could have? Did you ever see him get violent with her? Or hear anything that sounded like it?"

She took a deep breath and studied me through narrowed eyes. It took her a minute, but she finally answered. "Georgina gave just as good as she got."

"Was she violent with him?"

"I wasn't in their house, but as far as I know, nobody hit anybody. That doesn't mean they didn't rough each other up a little, only that I never heard anything that made me think they did. They'd scream and slam doors and call each other every name in the book and out of it, but that's all I know."

"Okay, thank you. I appreciate you talking to me."

"Even if she could cuss like a sailor, she didn't deserve to die like that. She was a real nice girl, that Georgina, to everyone but him. She didn't deserve that."

It was more or less the same thing the other couple of people I managed to talk to said. No one answered at most of the doors I tried. One person had only moved in after Georgina moved out. But the neighbor on the other side and the one across the street both answered and remembered Alex and Georgina's fights. From what they said, they were hard to forget—yelling and screaming, swearing and insulting, sometimes late into the night. No one ever saw either of them raise a hand to the other. No one ever saw any suspicious bruises. No one ever saw or heard anything to make them think that anything was going on but some vigorous screaming. It was time to go see Alex.

I turned to walk toward downtown, but as I passed Alex's house, I stopped and looked at it. On a whim, I walked up and knocked on the door. I was about to give up and go find Alex's office when the door opened. A man who resembled the creepy guy at the café who Sammy had identified as Alex stood there. That man, though, had been clean-shaven, neatly groomed, and well dressed. This guy wore a dirty-looking holey old T-shirt with sweatpants. His hair stuck out from his head in clumps that pointed off in different directions, and he had about three days of stubble on his chin.

"Alex?" I asked cautiously.

He nodded or at least made a movement with his head that I could interpret as a nod. "You're Fran from the coffee shop. That was a good latte."

"Thank you. Um..." I paused and looked at his red-rimmed eyes. "Are you okay?"

He rubbed his hand over his chin and then over his head, shifting his hair into a new indefinable shape. "Yeah, um, my girl-friend—my ex-girlfriend, I mean—"

"Georgina?"

"Yeah. You know?"

I nodded. "Everyone knows."

Alex slumped against the door. "I can't believe it. I mean, Georgie—" If it was possible, he leaned even harder against the door. I was worried he would slip to the ground if he didn't sit down.

"Can I come in? Could we maybe talk for a minute?"

He pushed himself up into a nearly vertical position. "Yeah. It's kind of a mess, but—"

Kind of didn't quite cover it. There were three open pizza boxes on the coffee table, two completely empty and one with one slice left in it. Empty beer and energy drink cans were scattered across the floor. A pillow and a blanket were balled up on the couch, and the TV was on a sports channel with the sound muted. Alex practically fell down onto the couch.

"I haven't really felt like cooking since I found out about Georgie," he said by way of explanation. From what I could see of the other rooms in the house, they didn't look like a bachelor pad exploded, so I was inclined to believe him. "You can sit down if you want."

I picked a couple of beer cans up off a chair and set them on the coffee table next to one of the pizza boxes. I perched myself on the edge of the chair. I wasn't sure if any of the contents of the cans had spilled, and I didn't exactly want my butt soaked in beer, so I figured it was safest that way.

"So, um, when did you find out about Georgina's death?" I asked, not sure how else to start the conversation.

"Late Tuesday afternoon just before I left work. One of the girls in the office had run an errand and saw the police tape around the jewelry store. When she came back in, she told me about it since she knew Georgie worked there. I tried to call Georgie's cell phone, but no one answered. A couple minutes later, some cop showed up at the office and told me Georgie was—Georgie was—" He closed his eyes and shook his head from side to side. A tear slipped down one cheek and got buried in the stubble. He was either an incredible actor or he was genuinely devastated by Georgina's death. I was pretty sure it was the latter.

"Alex," I said softly after giving him a minute to regain his composure.

He looked at me with eyes that looked as though the light had gone out of them.

It was the same look Matt's eyes had right after his dad died.

"Alex," I took a deep breath to get the next part out. "Did you kill Georgina?" It was more direct than I'd ever planned to be, but Alex seemed so broken and empty I couldn't stand to draw it out.

He looked like someone had punched him in the gut. I supposed it wasn't far from the truth. "You think I could have killed her?"

"You were seen arguing with her. Loudly. A lot."

"We weren't getting along anymore. That's why we broke up."

"You were seen arguing with her after you broke up too."

"I was just worried about her. She moved out. She didn't have anywhere to go. I offered to let her stay here, and I'd go stay with my parents or something, but she wouldn't do it. She said she didn't want to spend another second in the house she'd lived in with me." He looked up at me with grief-stricken eyes. "Can you believe she hated me that much? She'd rather be homeless than live in the house she'd lived in with me." He closed his eyes again and dropped his chin to his chest. "I even tried renting her an apartment a couple months ago—one of those above the shops on Main Street. I told her it would be just for her. I wouldn't even have a key. But she wouldn't go near it. I eventually gave up and moved my business in there. We'd been working out of here, but I signed a year-long lease on the place, and if Georgie wasn't going to move in, I didn't think it made sense to let it sit there empty. I told her that if she ever changed her mind, we'd move the business back in here, but—I guess that will never happen now."

Well, that certainly seemed like a plausible explanation for why Alex had moved his company onto Main Street. Maybe he hadn't done it to spy on Georgina the way Dean thought he was doing—unless he was lying, of course. I looked over at him again. For the first time, I noticed he had a picture of himself and Georgina on the coffee table. That's what he kept looking at with that heartbreaking expression. I couldn't believe he was lying.

"Where was Georgina staying? Do you know?"

"Different places. She'd crash at a friend's place for a night or two and then move on. She stayed at the jewelry store a lot of times."

"She what?" I asked, not believing my ears.

"She slept at the jewelry store. On a little couch in the back."

I remembered the pillow and blanket that had been on the couch in Dean's back room. That was where Georgina was sleeping? "Did Dean know?"

"Of course he did. She set the motion detector off a bunch of times at night, and the cops came out. Dean had to have the alarm company stop calling the police and call him instead."

"I have to go." I stood up.

"Okay," Alex said without moving.

I was halfway to the door when I stopped and turned around. "Alex?"

"Yeah?"

"Where were you Sunday night?"

He looked like he was going to be sick. "Speed dating. I was trying to get out there. I can find the address of the place if you want."

"No thanks. I won't need it." Alex was off my suspect list.

Chapter Sixteen

I was at Howard Jewelers so quickly I might as well have run there. I went straight around the back and punched the buzzer by the door. Banging my fist on the door, I looked straight into the camera. "Dean! Dean! Open the door, Dean! Dean! Open! The! Door! Dean! Now! Dean!" I almost punched him in the face when he finally opened it.

"Fran! What is it? Is something wrong?"

I pushed past him into the back room. "You'd better believe there is! That's what's wrong!" I pointed at the pillow and blanket still piled on one end of the couch.

"What? What do you mean?"

"You knew Georgina was sleeping here! That's why she was here that night. That's why the alarm company didn't call the police."

Dean looked sheepish, but I was so angry I didn't care.

"You lied to me! You asked me to help you, and then you lied to me."

"I didn't lie. I—"

"It's still a lie if you leave out important information, Dean!"

"I'm sorry. I just didn't think it was important. I—"

"I knew there was something wrong about your story. I knew it. I knew you were hiding something from me. But do you know what I thought it was? I thought you killed her! I thought you killed her, and you were blaming Alex to throw me off the trail. Why did you do that, Dean? Why?"

"I—I just—"

"You just what?" I knew it didn't make any sense to scream at him. I knew I was being irrational, but I felt like he'd used me, tricked me into investigating Georgina's death. But for what reason? What did he have to gain by sending me on a wild goose chase?

"I didn't think it was relevant."

"You didn't think the reason she was at your store hours after closing was relevant?"

"Well, you didn't ask, so..."

"Did the police ask?"

"Yes."

"And what did you tell them?"

"I said I..." He mumbled whatever he was saying so low I couldn't make it out.

"What?"

"I said I didn't know."

"Why, Dean? Why would you say that?"

"Because..." Again with the mumbling.

"Speak clearly, Dean."

"Because the insurance company would've had a fit. If they found out she was staying here and that the alarm company didn't call the police, they would reject my claim. That's a lot of money, Fran! I can't be out fifty thousand dollars!"

"You lied to me and to the police so that you wouldn't get in trouble with your insurance company."

"Yeah, basically."

"You're an idiot, Dean."

"What? Fran, I—"

"Stop it, Dean. Did you even actually think that Alex was responsible?"

"I thought it was possible."

"But not likely."

He shrugged.

"Please tell me you asked me to investigate because you actually wanted Georgina's killer brought to justice."

"Well, yeah." He didn't sound too sure about that.

"Why did you really ask me?"

"The police seemed..." More mumbling.

"Speak clearly!"

"The police seemed really focused on the robbery angle. I was afraid I looked like the most obvious suspect, and I'd either get arrested, or they'd never find a better suspect. If that's what the police came up with, that's probably what the insurance investigators would come up with, and then they wouldn't pay out."

"So you sent me after Alex and hoped the police would follow me."

"Well, you figured out who committed the other ones. I figured the police would have faith in you."

"Even if there was no evidence?"

He shrugged. I resisted calling him an idiot again.

"Did you do it, Dean?" At that point, I wouldn't have been surprised if he'd said yes. He was staging the robbery and accidentally killed Georgina in the process, so he thought he'd cover it up by pinning it on her ex-boyfriend. I hoped the security cameras recorded audio.

"No."

I stared at him and waited.

"I didn't kill Georgina."

I kept staring.

"You have to believe me, Fran! I didn't kill her! I didn't do it!"

"Whatever, Dean." I started for the door.

"Really, Fran! I didn't! Please believe me!" He reached out to grasp my arm as I walked by. I shook him off.

"Don't touch me."

"Fran, please!"

My hand was on the door. "I don't think you did it, Dean. This whole story is too stupid. I don't think you could have pulled it off."

I opened the door and walked out of the jeweler's and straight to my café. I maintained enough self-control to go around the back. I was too frustrated to smile and make nice with the customers I'd pass if I went in the front. I pulled open the back door, kicked the doorstop out of the door between the storage room and the café, and flopped down in my desk chair. I had no idea where to go from here. I had ruled out all my suspects on the basis of apathy, melancholy, or stupidity. I had no one left. In theory, my choices were to give it up or start over, but in reality, there was only one. I was going to start over.

"Fran! You're here." Rhonda came in.

"Yes," I grumbled.

"What's wrong?" She came over and bent to look at my face.

"Dean's an idiot."

"I could have told you that."

"And I have no suspects left."

"Well, that's new." She sat on the edge of the desk. "Dean's out?"

"He's a liar and an idiot."

"Alex?"

"Heartbroken and has an alibi."

"Umm..."

"Yeah, me too." She was out of ideas, and so was I.

"So what are you going to do?"

"Start over, I guess."

"You leave for Italy in four days."

"So I'll have to solve it by then."

"Fran—"

"I know, Rhonda, but I can't just forget about it. Georgina's dead. If there's anything I can do to catch her killer, I have to do it."

"You need a break."

"I'm going to Italy for two weeks."

"No, now. Well, tomorrow. How about that shopping trip?"

"Rhonda—"

"No, seriously, Fran! Getting away, even if it's just for a few hours, will be good for you. You said before that you needed things to wear on your trip. This is the perfect opportunity. Besides, it'll be a good morale boost for us before we slave away in your absence for two weeks."

It seemed so irresponsible to skip out on work for an afternoon. But I was so tired from everything that had gone on the past few days that it was really tempting.

"We can go to Neiman's!" she sing-song-ed.

"I told you I can't afford Neiman's."

"We can go there anyway!"

I actually laughed a little. "Okay, fine. Maybe it'll be fun."

"Of course it will! And trust me. You'll be thanking me later!" She hopped off the desk and headed back into the café.

As it turned out, I would.

Chapter Seventeen

The next afternoon, the five of us—Rhonda, Sammy, Becky, Amanda, and me—gathered in the coffee shop. The last customer had been served. Everything had been cleaned up. The sign in the window said "Closed," and the one next to it explained that Antonia's Italian Café would be closed on Friday afternoon for a team-building exercise. "Team-Building" also known as shopping.

"Okay, anything else?" Rhonda sounded more than a little exasperated that we still hadn't left for Boston.

"Oh, I need to get a latte for Ryan!" Sammy put her purse down on the counter and ran around it to the espresso machine. "I promised I'd bring him one!"

"Oh, for Pete's sake," Rhonda muttered.

"May as well get one for Mr. Stanton too." Becky giggled.

It took me a second to realize who she was talking about. Stanton, Detective Stanton, Mike—I was used to hearing him called all of those. Mr. Stanton somehow sounded strange, probably because it made me think of when I used to call his father that when we were kids.

"We're going to need more than one if we're going to get Mike through the whole afternoon," Rhonda said.

"I'll make it for him." I put my bag down and joined Sammy behind the counter. Mike has never been seen drinking any coffee that isn't strong and black, so I put on a pot for him.

Rhonda rolled her eyes as I made the fresh coffee and dropped her purse off her shoulder onto one of the tables. "May as well get a refill." She rattled the ice in her otherwise empty cup of iced tea.

"Get yourselves something, girls," I said to Becky and Amanda, knowing they wouldn't help themselves unless I told them to.

Their eyes lit up, and they went straight for the dessert case like I knew they would. They each pulled out a giant cupcake and a soda from the refrigerator.

"I miss having that metabolism." Rhonda looked longingly at their cupcakes.

When Mike's coffee was ready, I poured it out into three large to-go cups.

Becky giggled when she saw it. "Wow, you're really taking him three cups?"

I shrugged. "I'm taking three cups to the police department. If Mike wants to drink all three, he can. If he wants to drink one and give the other two away—" Rhonda laughed behind me. "He's welcome to do that too."

Before she put the lid on, I caught sight of the design Sammy had poured into Ryan's latte—a heart. I glanced at Rhonda to see if she'd seen it too. She wagged her eyebrows at me, and I knew that she had. Neither of us said anything to Sammy.

She put Ryan's latte into the last of the four slots in the drink carrier.

"Can somebody grab my purse?" I picked up the drinks.

"I got it!" Becky chirped.

I carefully balanced the many cups of hot coffee as we went outside to pile into Rhonda's minivan. Sammy locked up the shop, and I slid into the front seat. "Please drive carefully," I said as Rhonda put the car in gear.

"Not looking for a lap of hot coffee?" she asked.

"Not looking to spend the next couple weeks in the burn unit."

She drove very carefully over to the police station, managing to only make the coffee slosh out the slightest bit. She pulled into a spot labeled "Reserved for Officers" and shifted into park. "You need help getting out?" She punched the button on my seat belt so I wouldn't have to maneuver around the coffee to do it.

"I'll help her." Sammy practically jumped out of her seat in the back.

Rhonda and I exchanged a look. Neither of us was surprised.

Sammy opened my door for me and took the coffee carrier. I almost let her go in by herself, but Rhonda shoved me out of the car. "Don't let her think she's being sneaky."

"Are Sammy and Ryan, like, together?" I heard Becky ask as I climbed out of the car.

"Not according to Sammy," Rhonda replied.

"She sure doesn't act like it," Becky said as I closed the door.

"Hold up," I called to Sammy as I hurried to catch up.

I thought I saw a look of disappointment cross her face as she glanced back, but she slowed down until I was beside her.

Margaret Robbins, the talkative one, was at the desk when we walked in. "Special delivery?"

"Mm-hmm. For Officer Leary," Sammy said.

"And Detective Stanton." I caught Margaret's eye. Sammy didn't see her wink at me.

"They're in the conference room right here." Margaret pointed to her right. "If they're not, they'll be back in just a sec."

Sammy and I went over into the room Margaret had pointed to. My eye immediately went to a row of plastic bags laid out on one of the tables. I wandered over while Sammy pulled Ryan's latte out of the carrier and checked to make sure the image still showed in the milk foam.

I started looking at the bags–some pieces of glass, some small rocks that looked like they came from the sidewalk, a cordless phone. And there, at the end, something with a dark brown stain on it that looked suspiciously like a brick.

I hesitated but walked over to look at it more closely. It was definitely a brick, a relatively thin, tan brick, with what I could only assume was a bloodstain on it. Something about it seemed odd to me, even beyond the fact that it was stained with the blood of a woman I considered my friend. I reached out my hand. The brick was in a plastic bag. It couldn't hurt anything to touch it, right?

"One of those had better be for me," Mike said. I looked up to see him striding into the room. He stopped dead when he saw me with my hand outstretched toward his evidence bag. He looked at me with an expression that seemed to ask if I was really doing what he thought I was doing. I pulled my hand back and put it in my pocket. He nodded curtly and walked over to the coffee. He reached out to grab one, but Sammy snatched it away.

"That's, um, it's Ryan's." She stammered like she was doing something wrong. Mike hadn't moved his hand yet. I wondered how rough his day must have been to be looking at her that way over a cup of coffee when there were three more still sitting on the table.

"It has milk in it," I said quickly.

"Ugh." He grunted and moved his hand toward one of the others. "These safe?"

"Made fresh just for you," I said. "I personally made sure not a drop of milk or sugar came near any of them."

"Good." He picked one up.

"I left a little room in the top of each in case someone else wanted some."

"Someone else?" He flicked his eyes at Sammy.

"Anyone you might want to share with," I said.

He moved closer to the two remaining cups. "Every man for himself on a murder case."

I laughed even though I didn't think he was joking. I would not want to be the one to come between Mike Stanton and a cup of coffee.

"All right!" Ryan came into the room. "You're the best, Sam! Thanks!" He started toward Sammy with his arms out but stopped when he saw Mike and me. "Uh, I appreciate it. How much do I owe you?" he asked, suddenly much more reserved.

"Cops drink free, Leary," Mike growled.

Ryan nodded and took his cup from Sammy without trying to hug or pay her.

"Thanks for stopping by, ladies," Mike said. "But if you don't mind, we have an investigation to get back to."

"Not a problem," I said. "We have a shopping trip to get to. Plus, we've been gone more than thirty seconds now. Rhonda's probably about to send out a search party. You don't want to get between her and Neiman's."

"Don't tell me you're closed for the rest of the day." Mike looked pained.

"Why do you think I brought you three cups of coffee?"

"That'll get him through the next hour," Ryan said. "But what is he going to do the rest of the day?"

"Very funny, Leary," Mike said. "I think the ladies said they need to get going."

I headed for the door while Sammy and Ryan made little gestures like they wanted to hug but didn't want to be seen hugging.

"See ya, Mike!" I called over my shoulder as I walked back into the lobby.

"See ya, Fran! Thanks for the coffee!"

"No problem!" I waited a second to see if Sammy was behind me. She wasn't. "You coming, Sammy? Do I need to send Rhonda after you?"

"I'm coming!" She popped out of the room, turning around once to wave at Ryan before following me back out to the car.

"Sheesh, did you two take long enough?" Rhonda asked.

The doors were barely closed when she put the car in reverse. Neiman's was calling. She put her arm behind my seat so she could twist around to look behind us as she backed up. She caught my eye when I glanced over at her. I tried not to laugh out loud as she flicked her eyes from Sammy over to the police station and made kissy faces. I had to look away and cover my mouth so Sammy didn't notice. If she and Ryan just said they were seeing each other, we wouldn't joke about it so much. It was just the fact that they tried to pretend there was nothing between them when there so clearly was that made us tease them.

"You get the boys safely caffeinated?" Rhonda pulled out onto the road.

"Well, I'm not sure Mike consumes caffeine at safe doses, but we got it to them," I said.

"Did Mr. Stanton say if he was going to share?" Becky asked from the way back where she sat with Amanda. Sammy had the middle row of the minivan all to herself.

"I believe his exact words were 'every man for himself on a murder case,'" I told her.

"Does that mean no?"

Even Sammy laughed at that.

"Yes, that means no, Becky," I said.

We chatted as we pulled onto the highway and didn't stop until we reached Boston.

I already knew Sammy and Rhonda pretty well, but I learned exponentially more about Becky and Amanda in that hour and a half than I'd known before. Becky babysat for Mike's kids, which was part of why she called him Mr. Stanton. Amanda was just starting her junior year in high school, but she was already taking advanced chemistry and was planning on working as a cosmetic chemist after college. She went into incredible detail, explaining to us the chemical reaction that took place when coffee beans were roasted. I had no idea she was so smart.

Rhonda pulled into the parking lot near the Neiman Marcus, and we piled out of her van. She made a beeline for the store and was halfway across the parking lot before the van doors were closed.

"Come on, girls!" She pointed her key fob over her shoulder and locked the car as we followed her out into the street.

Inside, she led us straight to the women's clothing section. "Fran needs some new clothes for her trip. You girls can help us look or go do your own thing, and we can meet up later."

Becky and Amanda looked at each other and shrugged. "It's okay if we just meet you later?" Becky asked.

"Yes, but if you get lost, your mothers will kill me, so don't get lost, okay?"

"Okay."

I had a momentary bout of panic thinking about anything happening to either of them. They were my employees. I was responsible for them. Their mothers had entrusted them to me. I took a deep breath and tried to put the thought out of my head.

"You have all our cell phone numbers?" Rhonda asked.

"Yup."

Rhonda narrowed her eyes and studied both girls. I guessed that she was using her mom powers to scrutinize them for any plans for teenage shenanigans. Eventually, she nodded. "You have to meet up with us for dinner."

"No problem!"

Of course it was no problem. I was paying, and I'd promised them a decently nice restaurant. I had no doubts they'd show up wherever we told them to and probably fifteen minutes early. Unless something horrible happens to them. But I took another deep breath and reminded myself that I wasn't going to think about that.

"All right, off with you!" Rhonda waved her hands at them. "Go, have a good time. And I expect you to check in by text every hour."

"Okay!" Becky called as she and Amanda turned and walked away.

"Is it really okay to let them go off on their own like that?" I asked Rhonda nervously.

"You let them handle money and hot coffee, but you're worried about letting them wander around a department store on their own?" Rhonda asked.

"Yes."

"Fair enough. But, yes, I think they'll be fine. They're smart, competent girls. And it's not like they're six years old." She turned and eyed the racks of clothing. "Now, stop worrying about that. We have shopping to do!"

Rhonda led Sammy and me through the racks, heading in the direction of the clearance section. I was grateful. I had looked at a price tag or two as we walked and almost choked. I showed one to Sammy, and her big blue eyes got even bigger.

"That's a typo, right?" she whispered. "They put the decimal point in the wrong place?"

Even in New York, I hadn't bought clothes that cost that much money.

At the sale rack, Rhonda started picking garments up and slinging them over her arm.

"Rhonda, I–"

"It's fine. I'm just shopping," she said without so much as pausing in her perusal of the racks. "I'll pick some things up, you'll try them on. If they look gorgeous and chic and Italian, you'll buy them. Simple as that."

"She would make a great personal shopper," Sammy said.

"Too bad we don't have a Neiman's in Cape Bay," I replied.

"She'd spend everything she made."

"You think she doesn't now?"

Sammy laughed. "She has picked up some cute stuff for you."

I couldn't disagree even though I worried about the prices even on clearance. Rhonda wound her way through the racks for a few more minutes before declaring it time for me to try things on.

"I don't think they'll let me take all that in the fitting room," I said.

"It's fine. I'll swap things out for you as you try them on."

I looked at Sammy for help, but she giggled at my predicament. I gave in and shrugged. "All right, give me the first batch."

Rhonda pulled the first eight pieces off her pile, barely making a dent in it, and handed them to me. "Here you go! And don't forget to come out and show Sammy and me everything you try on, okay?"

"I'll show it to you if it looks good."

"Everything!" Rhonda repeated.

I was afraid enough of her deciding she would just camp out in the dressing room with me that I agreed. Approximately twenty-four outfits later, I finally put on something that Rhonda liked. I wasn't sure about it, but Rhonda loved it.

"I don't know." I looked at myself in the mirror outside the dressing room. "It's not really—"

"Black enough?" Rhonda asked.

The dress had a black-and-white floral pattern, and I had to admit it was the white that threw me off. The cut was fine. The fit was fine. But the presence of the white and the pattern made me uneasy.

"It really does look good on you, Fran," Sammy said.

I turned and looked at myself from the side. "I don't know if it looks Italian enough."

"The designer is Italian," Rhonda said.

"That doesn't mean it's something Italian women would wear."

"Haven't we been through this?" Rhonda asked Sammy.

Sammy nodded, although she looked a little reluctant.

"You're Italian, Fran," Rhonda said. "And you're wearing it. That means it's something Italian women would wear."

"But—" I was interrupted before I could say anything else.

"Francesca? Francesca, darling, is that you?" A familiar voice came from a few racks over.

"Mrs. D'Angelo?" Sammy whispered.

I nodded.

"Oh boy," Rhonda muttered.

"Francesca! It is you!" Mrs. D'Angelo announced, loud enough for the entire store to hear. "And Samantha! And Rhonda! How lovely to see you all here. What a remarkable coincidence!" She grabbed both my hands in hers. "And you look lovely, Francesca! Are you thinking of buying that dress? You should! It's quite slimming."

I glanced down at my body and wondered if slimming was something I needed to worry about.

"What are you all doing here? Are you shopping for Francesca? That's lovely, so lovely." She turned her attentions to Sammy, much to my relief. My nose had started to stuff up as a defense against her intense floral perfume. "Are you going to get some shopping in too, Samantha? Oh, you should! It never hurts to spruce up your wardrobe a bit! Don't you forget that either, Rhonda! You know as we get older, we have to start dressing more maturely, but that doesn't mean we have to be unfashionable. We have to maintain ourselves! Keep ourselves looking young! And sprightly!"

She waved one hand around in the air as she spoke. As usual, I was struck by how long and red her fingernails were. At least this time, they weren't digging into my arm as she counseled me on something I didn't know I needed to be counseled on.

"What time is it?" she asked, without skipping a beat. Before any of us could say anything, she turned her wrist to look at her gold wristwatch. "Oh, my! I must be going! I have an appointment with that Diane Bernard to see about having my front walk redone, and if I don't leave right now, I won't have time to freshen up before she arrives. Such a sourpuss, that one! Her and her sister both! What's her sister's name?" Whether it was a rhetorical question or she just remembered the answer, she plowed on. "That's it! Sabine! Sourpusses, aren't they? But Diane does such lovely work. I've asked her to do it in brick—something classic, a herringbone pattern perhaps. In any case, I must be off if I'm to be ready to meet her! Goodbye, ladies!" She disappeared off through the racks without any of us having a chance to say a word to her.

"Does my wardrobe need sprucing up?" Sammy held out her shirt. "I mean, I know this is an old shirt, but I didn't think it looked bad."

"What about me?" Rhonda asked. "A seventy-five-year-old woman just announced to all of Neiman's that I was getting old and needed to maintain myself! We need to hit the skincare counter before we get out of here. Are you going to buy that dress, Fran? You need to. It's perfect."

"Um, I don't know." Mrs. D'Angelo's words rang in my ears.

"Come on!" Rhonda said. "Buy it! It looks so good!"

I agreed numbly. The rest of the afternoon, I felt like I had earmuffs on. I barely heard a word anyone said through our skin counter trip and our dinner and our drive home. I waved goodbye to Becky and Amanda as Rhonda dropped each of them off at their houses, but I'd been so distracted, I'd practically forgotten to be relieved when they rejoined us at dinner.

"Are you okay, Fran?" Sammy asked after they got out of the car.

"Yeah, um, just a little..." I trailed off as I touched a hand to my head.

"Tired? Headache-y? Distracted thinking about wearing that dress as you wander the streets of Rome on Matt's arm?" Rhonda offered.

I managed a smile and a nod. "Yes."

I couldn't tell them that what really had me so distracted was that I knew who'd killed Georgina.

Chapter Eighteen

When I woke up in the morning, for a few glorious seconds, I didn't think anything about what I'd realized the day before. Then it all came rushing back to me, and my heart raced in my chest. I couldn't stop thinking. It ran around and around in my head like a terrible song. *Diane killed Georgina. Diane killed Georgina. Diane killed Georgina.*

Even though I'd known all along that someone was responsible for Georgina's death, suddenly attaching a name to the words "Georgina's murderer" made me feel sick. And the fact that it was someone I–sort of–knew, had served in my café, and had, however briefly, spoken with made it even worse.

It was so obvious. I couldn't believe I hadn't put it together sooner. That brick, the one in the evidence bag with the bloodstain—it was too thin to be used on the exterior of a house.

But it was the perfect thickness for creating a decorative garden border or front walk. I'd held one before at the home improvement store and knew that it was still deceptively heavy. You wouldn't need to be a former quarterback to give that thing some heft and fling it through a window. I shuddered to think about what would happen if one slammed into your skull. Exactly what happened to Georgina, that was what.

And then there was Sabine with her perfectly designed brick front walk and the way she'd hesitated to tell me who did it for her. I'd known in my gut that it hadn't been there when she moved in. It was new, and her sister was the one who'd put it in. Her sister who was so grumpy and unpleasant. Her sister who had a perfect motive for breaking into the jewelry store—to "help" her sister's boyfriend get the perfect engagement ring. I had no doubt that the Diane I'd met had the nerves and the cold, hard edge to do it either. I just had to prove it.

I dragged myself out of bed. Latte was as excited to see me awake as ever. I welcomed the distraction, even if it only took a few minutes to let him outside and feed him.

I took a quick shower and stood in front of my closet, staring at my collection of clothing. What do you wear to confront a murderer? Not that I wanted to confront her. But I knew that if I went to Mike, or even Ryan, with my flimsy evidence, they'd send me on my way. Maybe they would look into it eventually, but that was precious time that Georgina's murderer would be walking free while her victim was quite literally cooling her heels in the county morgue.

I had to get Diane to confess. Failing that, maybe I could at least find some evidence. The ring would be ideal, but would that be somewhere that I could easily find it? Without breaking any laws? Of course, Mike had been careful to emphasize that I was not acting as an agent of the police. If I had been, I'd have to follow all their rules—rules like getting a search warrant before going through someone's house. So since he also made sure I knew I wasn't representing the police, maybe a little light breaking and entering wouldn't hurt? If it helped solve the case?

Probably not. Even if Mike would be able to use any evidence I found, he'd probably throw me in jail for as long as he could just to teach me a lesson about minding my own business.

I looked at my closet again. The day's agenda held, at a minimum, murderer confronting, evidence searching, probably not any breaking and entering—trespassing wasn't a crime unless somebody complained, right?—maybe a little climbing around in Diane's backyard? With any luck, I'd also be turning Diane over to the police and getting at least a solid pat on the back from Mike for my good investigative work. Maybe a reporter would take my picture for the newspaper. Okay, now I was dreaming. And I still needed to decide what to wear.

I decided you should look good to confront a murderer. Why not?

I pulled out my favorite pair of jeans and a cornflower-blue sweater that matched my eyes. I blew out my hair and curled it for the first time in ages. My hair was so heavy and thick that I kept it up most of the time while working in the café. I didn't need anything to make me any hotter than I already got working over the espresso machine. Curling it the way I used to when I lived in New York felt good though. Maybe I'd try to do it more often. Its dark color did make my eyes pop.

After I put on my makeup, I checked myself out in the mirror. Would this look intimidate Diane? Probably not. I didn't think much intimidated her, probably not even Mike. But at least I knew I'd look good.

I fished out a pair of practical, flat-heeled riding boots from my closet and pulled them on. Karen would have been disappointed, but at least I'd be able to walk without aerating the grass. Telltale heel holes wouldn't help me be stealthy while poking around at Diane's house.

Deciding I looked as good as I was going to, I headed downstairs to collect Latte for his walk. He jumped up and down, excited to head out. I felt bad that I was only going to take him around the block, but I needed to get to Diane's before my courage failed me.

Latte and I went out and started down the sidewalk toward Main Street. When we got to the corner where we usually turned left, I turned right in the direction of Diane's house. Latte got excited, thinking he was getting to go on an adventure.

But when we got to the next corner where we should have turned to circle back around to the house, I kept going straight. Latte's steps got even bouncier than usual as he realized he was definitely getting to go on an adventure. I was kind of glad I couldn't speak dog. It meant I didn't have to tell him that we wouldn't be going on an adventure and that I'd just decided to take a slightly longer walk than usual. I was pretty sure I was procrastinating. Either that or I was walking myself to Diane's. But Latte would be more of a hindrance than a help there, so I knew taking him was a bad idea.

We kept walking.

When we got to Diane's street, I turned. I told myself I just wanted to walk by and make sure I knew where it was. Then I'd take Latte home and come back on my own. It would be good for Latte to have such a nice, long walk. I watched the house numbers as we passed, looking for the one I'd found online the night before as I dug around researching Diane. When I came to it, I was surprised. The whole house was as neat and tidy as her sister's hadn't been. There was exquisite stonework outside, of course, even more impressive than what I'd seen at Sabine's, but on top of that, the house and yard were immaculately maintained. The house's white paint looked like it had been painted yesterday, and the blue on the shutters was so vibrant it almost glowed. The grass was a perfectly uniform height without a weed to be seen. I also had a feeling that I'd found the green thumb in the family, and it wasn't Sabine.

While Sabine's garden had been pretty with lots of fall color, Diane's garden was amazing. She had the most incredible array of flowers—in bloom, no less. There was an assortment of bushes with leaves in the process of changing color for the fall, brilliant reds, yellows, and oranges. I wondered what they were and where I could find them for my own garden. It was too bad Diane would be going to jail. I would have loved to hire her to landscape my yard. Based on the number of other plants I saw, I was pretty sure she had one of those amazing gardens with year-round color. I'd always wanted one of those. It was too bad I had no gardening skill whatsoever. I was pretty sure I could kill silk flowers. I wondered how hostile Diane was able to create something so beautiful. Or maybe I wondered how someone who created something so beautiful could be so hostile. Either way, I was baffled.

Something possessed me to turn up the front walk. *I'm just going to look*, I told myself right up until my finger pushed the doorbell. This one definitely worked. Not only was the little light lit up, I heard it ring loud and clear inside the house. I waited patiently, or as patiently as I could anyway, for Diane to come to the door. I counted to one hundred to make sure I wasn't rushing. I pushed the doorbell again. I counted to one hundred. Still nothing.

I decided that since she wasn't home, or at least was acting like she wasn't, it wouldn't be totally out of the question for me to look around a little bit—like I was a friend, checking on her, or a potential home buyer, one of those ones who goes up to houses that aren't even on the market and offers an astronomical sum to convince the owners to sell. *Although, if I was going to do that, I'd do it for one of the houses on the beach, not this one.* It was cute and all, but not so cute that I'd ever even consider paying three times the market rate for it in the imaginary world where I had that kind of money, of course.

I leaned over and looked in one of the windows next to the door. It was bright inside even though, as far as I could tell, the lights were all off. Diane had great natural light in the place. I didn't see any sign of Diane though. Or of the ring. I leaned over to the other window. More of the same. Latte pulled at his leash, bored by the inactivity.

"Shh," I whispered. "Stay. We'll go in a minute. I just want to look around a little." He calmed down but kept walking back and forth behind me, pulling his leash to its limit.

The other front windows were over the garden. It looked like there was space for me to walk down behind the plants, especially if I scooted down sideways. Latte would be a problem though. I didn't think I could wiggle my way back there without him trampling everything. Fortunately, he wasn't much of one for wandering off.

"Latte, you behave," I said quietly and dropped the leash. He seemed to listen to me and understand. He just took a couple of extra steps and sniffed a perfectly mowed section of grass. I hoped he wouldn't pee on it.

I sidled down behind the plants and looked in the first window. It was another room, also bright with sunlight. Based on the furniture, it looked like a very well-decorated living room because of course, the inside of her house would be as stunning as the outside. But other than that, I didn't see anything useful. No Diane, no ring. I made my way to the next one. Same room, but I scanned it carefully again in case I could spot something important. Nothing.

I peeked around the corner of the house to see if there were any windows. There were two more, probably still of the living room, but I wanted to look through them anyway. One was the living room, but the next was frosted over, and I couldn't see anything. It was either the ring-hiding room or the bathroom. The bathroom seemed a more likely candidate unless she was hiding the ring in the bathroom. But a bathroom seemed like a poor choice, too many drains to drop something small and incredibly valuable down.

I'd reached the tall privacy fence that encircled the backyard. I couldn't see through or over it. I tried jumping, but that didn't help, and I suspected it made me look even more suspicious than I probably already did. I walked back across in front of the house to look in the windows on the other side, passing Latte, who happily sniffed another section of the lawn. As long as he didn't start chewing on any of the plants, we were good.

The windows on the other side looked into what appeared to be a home office, probably where she managed the stonework business. Now that would be a good place to hide a ring. I looked around the room as much as I could from each window, getting up on my toes and leaning to the side to get as many angles as I could. I saw about a million places to hide a ring—boxes, drawers, filing cabinets, various pieces of furniture—but no actual ring.

The last window on that side looked into the kitchen. *Again, tons of places to hide a ring, but no visible ring.* And still no Diane. I drummed my fingers on the side of the house. I hadn't found anything useful yet, and short of that breaking and entering idea, I had nothing else to look at—unless I could get in the backyard.

I looked at the fence. No gate on this side and the neighbors had a fence too, so I couldn't circle around the back. I headed across in front of the house to check the other side. No gate there either. I went back out front to collect Latte and decide what my next move would be. When I came around the corner, I froze. Where was Latte? I jogged across in front of the house to check around the other corner. No dog. I turned around slowly. No dog. I turned again, quickly this time, in case he had managed to hide behind my back. No dog.

My heart pounded. Where was Latte? Where did he go?

"Latte!" I hissed in a loud whisper. I didn't want to actually yell and draw the neighbors' attention to my trespassing. "Latte!" I whispered again. I ran out toward the road and looked up and down Diane's street. No little tan dog. I looked back at the house, just in time to see his tail disappear around the corner on the living room/ bathroom side. I ran after him. "Latte!" I came around the corner of the house as his hind legs slid through a dip in the ground under the fence. Latte was in the backyard, the backyard that had no gate. If I wasn't panicking before, I was now.

"Latte! Latte!" I whisper-screamed. I got down on my belly to see if I could slide through the same spot. Not a chance. Even my head was too big. If I laid my head on the grass though, I could see through the little space and see Latte on the other side, happily sniffing. "Latte!" I whispered. He heard me. He looked up at me, panted a little with that doggy smile on his face, and went back to sniffing. *So much for the success of those obedience lessons.*

I stuck my arm through the hole. "Latte!" I called softly. I snapped my fingers and waved my hand. Nothing. He glanced my way and went back to what he was doing. I sat up and leaned against the corner of the house. What was I going to do? I was fairly certain that he would come out of there sooner or later. I was just afraid it was going to be much later rather than anything remotely resembling sooner. And Diane could come home at any minute. Who knew where she was or what she was doing? Hocking the ring, the only evidence, somewhere? That would be my luck.

I looked under the fence again. Latte was still sniffing. "Latte!" I called once more for good measure. No dice. I looked at the fence and wondered briefly if I could kickbox it down but quickly decided that calling it unlikely was an understatement. Then my eyes landed on the neighbor's yard. Where

Diane's lawn was completely unspoiled, the neighbors had gardening tools strewn about—garden gloves, a trowel, a rake... and a wheelbarrow. I knew what I was going to do. I was either going to break my arm or I was going to use the wheelbarrow to climb over the fence.

I checked if there was anyone walking down the street or any curtains twitching suspiciously in the windows. I was in the clear. I popped up and darted into the neighbor's yard. I grabbed the wheelbarrow and wheeled it over to the fence. I thought about flipping it over, but I'd probably end up stepping on the wheel and falling off.

I made sure my new stepstool was on fairly even ground then cautiously stepped one foot into it. It seemed steady. I braced myself against the fence and lifted my other leg in. So *far, so good.* From here, I could reach the top of the fence and see over it. There was Latte, still sniffing away. Holding on to the fence, I tried to swing a leg up to the top. *Nope, not a chance.* I looked down at the wheelbarrow. I didn't like my options, but I had to get my dog.

Still holding on to the top of the fence, I took a slow deep breath then lifted one foot and put it on the edge of the wheelbarrow.

It didn't tip. Gradually, I shifted my weight onto it.

Somehow, I didn't fall over. I tried again to swing my leg on top of the fence, and this time it worked. I decided it was probably a bad idea to jump down, so I worked my way up until I sat on the fence then dropped both legs over the other side. I pushed my feet against the fence in an effort to support weight and lowered myself down into the backyard. I had no idea how I was going to get back out, but that was something to worry about after I'd gotten hold of Latte.

"Latte!" I whispered. He still didn't care. He turned the corner of the house and walked onto, of course, a perfectly patterned brick patio. I hurried after him. As soon as I got to where I could see the whole backyard, I saw my way out. Well, my way out, and with any luck, my evidence against Diane—a neat pile of tan paving bricks, low enough that I could climb onto it, but high enough that I could get over the fence. And every one of the bricks was exactly like the one that smashed through the window of Howard Jewelers and killed Georgina.

I dashed across the yard to grab one of the bricks. I needed it to show Mike. Brick in hand, I ran for Latte.

"Latte, come here!"

I breathed a sigh of relief as, for once, he listened. I grabbed his leash and pulled him with me back toward the pile of bricks. Salvation was near.

"What are you doing here?"

I instantly wanted to throw up, cry, or hurl myself to the ground and scream. Instead, I acted like an adult and turned around.

How had I not seen her there? She stood at the backdoor of the house, looking calm and yet furiously angry. I tried to swallow, but it's hard when your mouth has completely dried up.

"Sabine."

"I asked you what you're doing here," Sabine said, her voice low and even and ice cold.

"I, um, accidentally dropped my dog's leash, and he ran into the backyard and—"

"You *accidentally* dropped your dog's leash so you could look into my sister's windows, you mean."

"Um..."

"Don't lie. I saw you."

My heart beat furiously in my ears. I wondered if I could make it to the pile of bricks and over the fence before she got to me. Probably if I was on my own, but not with Latte, and I definitely wasn't leaving him. My mind raced. What was I supposed to do? Apologize profusely? Beg forgiveness? Smile pretty and hope she'd just let me go? Not if she knew her sister was a murderer, she wouldn't, not with me holding an exact replica of the murder weapon in my hand. But if she didn't know...

"Sabine," I said quietly.

She glared, her eyes not showing the faintest trace of emotion. I took a step toward her. She didn't flinch.

"Sabine, Diane killed Georgina. With one of these." I held up the brick. "It was an accident, but she killed her."

"No," Sabine whispered.

"Yes. She knew how much you wanted that ring, and she wanted you to have it. You're her baby sister, and she loves you. She wanted you to be happy."

Sabine's eyes were huge, and I thought I saw tears welling up in her eyes.

"She made a mistake, a huge mistake, stealing that ring and killing Georgina. She wanted to do a good thing for you, but she ended up doing something very, very, incredibly bad. It was a mistake."

"No," Sabine whispered again.

"Yes. I'm sorry."

"No."

"Sabine, listen. Even though it was a mistake, she can't get away with it. It wouldn't be good for her, for you, for Cape Bay. Think of the guilt she'll feel for the rest of her life for taking Georgina's life. Her life, Sabine."

"No."

"Yes. She needs help–"

"She didn't do it."

"Yes, she did, Sabine. The evidence–"

"I did it."

I stopped cold. Was she telling the truth? Or was she lying to protect the sister who'd killed for her? "Sabine–"

"Stop it, Sabine!" I heard behind me. I whirled around. There was Diane, weapon of choice in hand, standing uncomfortably close to me.

"No, Diane. I won't let you go down for this!" Sabine looked at me. "I did it. I did it. I did it!" She got louder and louder each time. "I did it. I killed her! I killed Georgina. I wanted that ring, and I took one of Diane's bricks and threw it through the window. I killed Georgina!" By the end, she was yelling.

"Sabine, shut up!" Diane screamed. "What are you doing? What's wrong with you? Shut up, shut up, shut up!" She had gradually been moving closer to Sabine and was now so close to me that her yelling hurt my ears.

"No, Diane! No!"

"Damn it, Sabine!" Diane yelled back.

Latte started barking during all the shouting, and he hadn't stopped. I couldn't think with all the noise. All I knew was I had to get out of there before one of them turned on me. I had to talk them down.

"Okay, let's everybody take a deep breath," I said in as soothing a voice as I could muster.

"You!" Diane rounded on me. "This is your fault! They had no evidence! None!

Then you had to start sticking your nose where it doesn't belong! This is your fault!"

She raised the brick high over her head. She was so close to me, I couldn't avoid it. As the brick came down on my head, I flung the one I was holding toward Diane, knowing that I couldn't save myself, but hoping to at least hurt her before I went down.

There was screaming. I heard sirens. Latte barked.

"Police! Police! Police! Drop the weapon! Down on the ground!" I saw Mike's face over me, frantically pushing the hair back from my face with his blood-covered hands. I wondered whose it was. Had he gotten hurt somehow? "Franny! Franny! Fran! Stay with me! Franny! Francesca!" The last thing I saw was the panic in his eyes. Everything went black.

Chapter Nineteen

Late Monday evening, I sat at a table toward the back of the darkened café. We had most of the lights off so we didn't look like we were open, but there wasn't much tourist traffic at that time of year or hour of night, so we probably could have had every light on and as long as the sign on the door said "Closed," no one would have bothered us.

"You need a refill, Mike?" Rhonda stood up.

For what I guessed was the first time in his life, Mike declined a cup of coffee. "No, I've got to be up early in the morning."

Sammy's mouth dropped open. Rhonda leaned over and felt his forehead before he swatted her away.

"I need to see if you have a fever!" She reached for his forehead again. He swatted some more. "Just be glad I don't do it the way I do it for my kids."

"Don't you dare kiss my forehead!"

"Oh, Sandra does that too?" She grinned at him.

He rolled his eyes and wiggled his to-go cup of coffee in his hand. "Not empty anyway."

"A half-full cup has never stopped you before. Anyone else?" She looked at the rest of us.

"I'll take another latte," Ryan said. "Unlike Stanton here, I'm working second shift tomorrow."

Rhonda nodded.

"Some ladyfingers?" Sammy asked.

Rhonda nodded again. "Anybody else?"

"Chocolate cupcake!" Matt said.

"Coming up. Fran?"

I shook my head. I still didn't feel much like eating. Besides, I figured I'd get more than my fill in Italy. I'd be hungry by then.

Rhonda walked over behind the counter and got Sammy's ladyfingers and Matt's cupcake and brought them back over to the table. Then she went to make Ryan's latte.

Despite the stresses of keeping the café running, the sound of the espresso machine was soothing. It was a sound I'd heard every day of my childhood and almost every day of my life. In college, I'd sometimes go to the campus coffee shop just for the comforting sounds of coffee being prepared. It calmed me down when I was stressed and comforted me when I was anxious. During the stress of finals, I would go and study there because that sound made everything else disappear.

After the trauma of the past week, listening to Rhonda make Ryan's latte made me feel like everything was going to be all right. A two-week sojourn to Italy would no doubt raise my spirits even more.

Rhonda brought Ryan's fresh cup over to him, took the old one into the back to be washed, then grabbed the pitcher of iced tea from the refrigerator to refill her glass. She sat down, leaving the pitcher on the table.

Sammy picked up one of her ladyfingers and dipped it in Ryan's latte before taking a bite. Rhonda raised her eyebrows and looked pointedly from Ryan's cup to Sammy's mouth.

"Oh, stop!" Sammy exclaimed. "You can't exactly dunk ladyfingers in a glass of water, can you?"

"I would have made you your own latte if you wanted," Rhonda said with an innocent look on her face.

"I don't need a whole one. I have to open this place up in the morning, remember?"

"I could have made you one just for dunking."

"I wouldn't want to waste the coffee," Sammy countered.

"I could have made a small one."

Sammy rolled her eyes and didn't say anything else. She was slowly learning that half the time, Rhonda was only giving her grief. I glanced at Mike and saw him look at Ryan and try not to smile. I looked at Ryan in time to see him shrug one shoulder. A smile pulled at one of the corners of his mouth. Mike took a swallow of his coffee. Rhonda looked at him, raised her eyebrows, and nodded. Mike smiled and shook his head.

I stared at my latte.

"So what *happened*?" Rhonda finally asked.

I leaned forward, propping my elbows on the table, and rubbed my face with my hands. Matt rested his hand on my back.

"You want the official story?" Mike asked.

"I'll take whatever story I can get at this point," Rhonda replied.

"Sabine Bernard threw a brick she obtained from her sister's stonework company through the side window at Howard Jewelers on Monday evening around ten p.m., hitting Georgina Rockwell in the head, causing Miss Rockwell's immediate death as a result of blunt force trauma. Miss Bernard climbed in through the window, stepping over Miss Rockwell's body, picked up the brick–"

"Which was covered in Georgina's blood," Ryan interrupted.

Mike gave him a dirty look. "Miss Bernard picked up the brick from beside Miss Rockwell's body and used it to smash the jewelry case where a diamond ring valued between fifty and seventy-five thousand dollars was stored. Miss Bernard took the ring and left the jewelers through the hole in the window. Dean Howard was made aware of the break-in by the alarm company, which was alerted by the initial glass break. When Mr. Howard arrived at the store, he found the broken window and Miss Rockwell's body and called the police." Mike finished his story by taking another sip of his coffee.

Rhonda held up her hands and applauded quietly. "Nice work. Very professional summary. Leaving out some of the important points at the end. Thanks anyway, Mike." She rotated in her chair to look at me. "Now, Fran?"

I sighed and rubbed my hands back and forth across my face again then leaned back in my chair.

"Sabine wanted the ring. She thought that if Sean loved her enough, he would have found a way to pay for it. If he didn't have the money, he could take out a loan, sell his car, sell whatever he could to get her what she wanted. Sean didn't have the money, couldn't qualify for a loan, didn't have enough to sell to get the money. She didn't care. She thought he should negotiate Dean down. Dean wouldn't go down. She finally got fed up and decided she was going to get the ring herself."

Rhonda exhaled sharply and shook her head. "And the rest?"

Matt pulled his arm tight around me as I leaned into him. I heard Mike take a ragged breath. When his voice came out, it was low and strained.

"Franny had enough circumstantial evidence that she thought Diane did it. She went to her house to try and find any kind of physical evidence that she could use to convince us that Diane was the killer."

"We know that part," Rhonda said.

"Rhonda," Sammy said, giving her a come-on look.

"Sorry," Rhonda said.

Mike took another deep breath. "One of the neighbors saw Fran climbing over the fence into Diane's backyard and called the police."

"Thank God," Rhonda said.

Matt held on to me even tighter.

"When we arrived on scene, we heard the screaming and went in through the house. By the time we got into the backyard, Franny—" He cut himself off and covered his mouth with his fist. If I didn't know better, I would have thought there were tears in his eyes.

"By the time we got into the backyard, Fran was on the ground." Ryan jumped in to save Mike from having to finish. "Mike went to her. Woodrow took down Diane, and Phillips got Sabine." He looked over at me and smiled. "I got Latte."

I gave him the best smile I could manage. I didn't like hearing the story over again. It brought back the image of Mike shouting and the blood on his hands and the terror in his eyes.

"You were so lucky to get away with a mild concussion." Rhonda reached across Matt to squeeze my hand. I gave her the same weak smile I'd given Ryan.

"Damn right she was. I told you not to—" Mike stopped, blinked hard, and stared at the wall. If I hadn't before, I knew now that at least half the reason he told me to stay out of his cases was to protect me. The rest of it was definitely that he didn't want me interfering with his investigations as much as I didn't want him interfering with my coffee.

"So what are they charged with? I know it was in the paper but—" Rhonda asked.

"Felony murder and possession of stolen goods for Sabine. Diane got attempted murder, assault with a deadly weapon, accessory after the fact, obstruction of justice..." Ryan thought for a second. "Did I miss anything?"

Mike shook his head.

"Mike kind of pushed the DA to throw everything he could at Diane. Some of the lesser ones will probably get dropped later."

Rhonda looked outraged, but Ryan cut her off before she could say anything. "It actually helps get a conviction on the higher counts. If they have the option to acquit a guilty guy or convict him of murder one, they'll convict. If they have the choice between murder one, murder two, or acquittal, they'll go for murder two. Juries are soft."

Rhonda nodded. I knew she wanted Diane in jail for as long as possible. She'd told me as much when she visited me in the hospital during my overnight-for-observation stay. She wanted Sabine in prison too, but it was personal with Diane. I suspected it was the same with Mike.

"The thing I still don't understand is," Sammy said, "what was she going to do with it? It's not like she could wear it around town without anyone noticing."

I shrugged. "Your guess is as good as mine."

Rhonda looked at Mike.

"I don't think she thought that far ahead," he said. "Maybe she just thought she'd wear it around the house or something?"

"For me, that's what's most tragic," Matt said. "She went to all this trouble, took someone's life, is probably—hopefully— going to jail for the rest of her life, and she wasn't even going to be able to wear the thing."

"What did she think Sean was going to think?" Sammy asked. "He wouldn't notice a fifty-thousand-dollar ring on his fiancée's hand?"

I shrugged again.

"You better believe I'd notice it if Sandra was suddenly walking around with a new luxury car on her hand," Mike said.

"Besides, have you seen that thing?" Ryan asked. All of us except Mike shook our heads. "Thing would blind you if you looked at it in sunlight. You could probably shine a flashlight at it and use it as a spotlight."

I'd only seen the picture, and I believed him, despite the look Mike gave him. I knew

Mike disapproved of Ryan's editorializing about the case and the ring, but also that it couldn't bother him too much since he kept Ryan around. Not that he would fire him over something like that, just that he wouldn't invite him to work on the big cases or socialize with him. It was obvious that Mike had taken Ryan under his wing, and I guessed that the looks he kept giving him were more to help guide him than to chastise him. Still, it was fun getting the extra details Ryan liked to provide—when they didn't involve bloody murder weapons anyway.

"Where was she even keeping it?" Rhonda asked.

"In a box of old clothes in the back of her closet. Loose. She could have lost it just by forgetting which sweater it was tucked into and shaking it out," Mike said.

"So she couldn't even look at it," Rhonda said.

"Nope," Mike replied. "Not unless she wanted to play contortionist and climb over the fifty or so other boxes she had in there."

Rhonda shook her head like she was mourning the invisibility of the ring Sabine had gone to so much trouble to steal. No one else said anything either. I was thinking about the senselessness of it all, and I assumed they were too.

"Are you two excited about your trip?" Rhonda asked Matt and me after a respectable lull in the conversation.

Matt's face lit up immediately, and I couldn't help smiling. I was already excited, but his excitement ramped it up even more. I loved spending time with him no matter where we were, but spending two whole weeks in Italy with him would be incredible. And knowing that he was thrilled to spend that time with me practically made my heart flutter in my chest.

"Oh, I can't wait!" Matt said.

"Have you planned out your wardrobe for every second of the trip?" she asked him.

His forehead wrinkled up. "No?" He glanced at me. "Was I supposed to?" I shook my head.

"This one has." She jerked her thumb at me. "She has put more thought into her wardrobe for this vacation than you would believe."

"Really?" He looked back at me.

"Only sort of," I said.

"You didn't know? Has she been hiding it from you? Fran, have you been wardrobe planning in secret again? Haven't we talked about this?" Rhonda leaned over to Sammy. "Do we need to stage an intervention?"

Sammy, to her credit, realized this time that Rhonda was messing with her and played along. "I don't know. We might."

"Fran," Rhonda said in a deadly serious tone of voice. She reached over and laid her hand on top of mine on the table. "Did you pack anything that wasn't black?"

I rolled my eyes and laughed. "Maybe one or two things."

"Good." She patted my hand. "Good." She leaned back in her chair and took a sip of her tea.

Sammy smiled and shook her head then looked over at Matt and me. "Fran's told me some, but what do you guys have planned?"

"Everything we can pack into two weeks," Matt said. "We're spending about three days in each of the cities we're going to."

"Is that enough time?"

"No!" I said adamantly.

Sammy laughed.

"It's enough to hit the highlights," Matt said. "We picked out a few places we really want to see in each city, so we'll go to those and then anywhere else we can fit in."

"It's so exciting, Fran! How do you stand it?" Sammy asked.

"I haven't been able to sleep for days. And not just because someone tried to kill me on Saturday."

"I *really* don't know how you stand that," Sammy said.

"You were lucky to get away alive. You know that, right, Fran?" Mike asked.

I nodded. "Trust me. I know." I really wasn't lying when I said that my anticipation of the trip was keeping me up at night, but it didn't help that when I did drift off, I saw Diane hovering behind me with a brick raised over my head. I would start awake, barely suppressing a scream and soaked in sweat.

It terrified me more now that it was over than it had when I was actually in the moment. It was probably a good thing, though, since when I woke up at night, I was frozen with fear. It took me five or ten minutes to calm myself down, which I'd usually do by thinking about the Italy trip.

That would get me excited, which would make it hard to fall back asleep, and the whole vicious cycle would start over again.

Mike looked like he wanted to say something else but didn't. I guessed he was trying not to lecture me yet again on leaving police work to the police, but that wasn't anything he had to worry about. I didn't plan on getting involved in any more murder investigations. In fact, I hoped I didn't even have the opportunity. It wouldn't hurt for Cape Bay to have its citizens stay safe and alive for a while.

"So, Mike..." Rhonda said.

Mike looked at her like he was expecting the worst. "Yes, Rhonda?"

"Out of curiosity—"

Mike rubbed his forehead as if whatever she was about to ask him was already hurting his head.

"How come Fran managed to solve this before you?"

Mike rubbed his head harder. He sighed and looked at Ryan. "Leary?" Apparently even Mike saw some benefit to Ryan's editorializing.

"Really?" Ryan asked.

"Why not?"

"All right." Ryan shrugged. He leaned forward and rested his forearms on the table. "So we pretty much eliminated Dean because he's not that much of an idiot. He's a lot of things, but not a total idiot. Even though Alex had a history with the vic—" He cringed and looked at me. "With Georgina, I mean, and he owned up to the two of them arguing, he was obviously pretty torn up about her death. We couldn't find anyone who had seen him around Georgina in the past few months. Besides, as Fran knows, he had a solid alibi. So we were working on Sean. His alibi was as weak as they come. 'Home alone with my girlfriend' is impossible to prove and is the same thing every lying murderer says. What we knew wasn't enough for a search warrant, so we were working the pawn shops and the fences and—"

"The fences? What does that mean? Like the fringes of society or something?" Sammy could be so adorably innocent sometimes.

"No," I said. "A fence is a person you take your stolen goods to so you can get rid of them. He pays you up front and then resells it. You get less money than you would have if you sold it yourself, but you don't get caught selling stolen goods either. They also say you're fencing the goods when you sell them to a fence."

"Wow, Fran," Rhonda said. "Do you have a little side business you'd like to tell us about?"

I laughed and turned back to Ryan. "Please continue."

"Basically, we knew the ring would be hard to get rid of. Like Sam said earlier, it's not as if he could give it to Sabine to wear around town. Everyone would notice it. So we were checking in with pawnshops and jewelers up and down the coast. Our best guess was that he'd try to sell it off somewhere out of town or overseas, but we couldn't find any evidence of Sean making contact with anyone who could have helped him. That's where we were—working the angles. Turns out Fran got lucky by not having the same resources we did. If she had, she might have gotten bogged down in the same details we did." Ryan raised his coffee cup to me in a toast.

"You have good instincts, Fran," Mike said.

"Thanks."

"It was a tough case though," Ryan said. "Obvious suspects, but almost no physical evidence anywhere. It's not like we can pull fingerprints off a brick to check against the system."

"Basically, we're lucky there's not still a murderer wandering the streets of Cape Bay," Matt said.

"She's got good instincts," Mike repeated.

We sat around and talked for a while longer before Mike got up to leave. "Sandra won't be happy if I'm not home to tuck the kids into bed." He slapped Ryan on the back and shook Matt's hand before he left. "Have a safe trip, man."

"Thanks," Matt replied.

"Franny." Mike turned to me. He opened his mouth then closed it. "Have a safe trip. Thanks again for your help, and if we ever have another murder, for Pete's sake, stay out of it."

I laughed. "Don't worry. I will."

"I'll believe it when I see it." He bent down to give me a hug.

"Thanks again for taking care of me," I whispered.

"No thanks necessary. It was just a concussion. I didn't do anything."

"You didn't know that though."

He looked at me and clenched his jaw a few times, looking like he was trying to control his emotions. We'd been friends for a long, long time, since we were kids, and I knew that when he saw me lying on the ground at Diane's house with blood pouring from my head, he'd thought that I was going to die in his arms. "Just doing my job," he said then turned back to the rest of the table. "Rhonda, thanks for the coffee. Sammy, I'll see you bright and early for another cup."

They waved goodbye, and Mike strode toward the door. A few feet from the trash can, he tossed his cup into it, getting it in cleanly.

"Nice shot!" Matt called.

Mike waved an acknowledgement over his shoulder and let himself out.

"I guess that's my cue to get out of here. Hopefully, Dan and the boys found something better to eat than Fritos for dinner again." Rhonda shook her head. "One of these days, I'm going to have to teach them to boil water. You'd think they could figure that out on their own, but they haven't succeeded yet." She said goodbye to everyone, gave me a hug, wished Matt and me *bon voyage*, then grabbed her jacket and headed out.

"Does that mean it's time for us to get going too?" Matt asked.

I yawned. "Yeah, probably."

"Will you be okay getting home, Sammy?" Matt asked just to make her answer.

"Yeah, I'll be okay."

"Are you sure? Franny and I can walk you if you want."

Sammy started to stutter as she tried to form the response we knew was coming.

Ryan jumped in and saved her. "It's out of your way. I'll walk her."

Sammy blushed and looked down at the table. She knew that we knew that her apartment was even farther out of Ryan's way than it was out of ours.

"If you guys want to go ahead, I want to talk to Sammy for a second," I said.

Sammy sunk farther down in her chair, probably afraid I was going to try to talk to her about the birds and the bees or something. Matt and Ryan graciously stood up and went to stand outside on the sidewalk.

"So, Sammy," I started, intentionally putting a tone in my voice that I knew she would interpret as starting a conversation about her relationship with Ryan.

"Yes?" Her face screwed up like she expected to hear the worst.

I dropped the teasing tone. "You've been working here for a few years now, right?"

She nodded. "Going on—" She tapped her fingers as she counted up the years. "Oh, wow, twelve years! I started when I was fifteen!"

"I knew it was a long time. How long have you had a key?"

She laughed. "Oh, at least ten."

"That's what I thought. You know, in a lot of places, only people in management are key holders."

She nodded slowly, looking like she was back to being afraid of where this was going. I wondered if I was dragging it out too long.

"And I think it's high time we fixed that."

She looked like she was going to cry. It was so like Sammy to be so humble as to assume I was going to take her key away. Definitely dragging it out too long.

"I think my mother never did this because she didn't put a lot of stock in titles, but Sammy?"

She nodded.

"You deserved to be made a manager a long time ago." I pulled the little stack of business cards I'd had made for her out of my pocket and pushed them across the table to her. There wasn't much use for business cards in running a small coffee shop in a coastal Massachusetts town, but I thought she'd appreciate the gesture.

She looked down at the stack printed with "Samantha Ericksen" and underneath that "Manager." Tears spilled down her cheeks. "Thank you!" She stood up to give me a big hug.

"Thank you for all your hard work." I hugged her back. "By the way, you can still take care of Latte while I'm gone, right?"

Sammy laughed. "Yes, of course. I'll be over in the morning to pick him up. And don't spend your whole trip worrying about him. I'll take good care of him."

I wasn't worried. I knew he and my café were in excellent hands.

Chapter Twenty

It seemed like a year later that I sat with Matt at a café table in the Piazza San Marco in Venice, but it had been just over a week since Sabine was arrested for Georgina's murder. I felt a world away from Cape Bay and the murder investigation, and I supposed that, in a way, I was. I was sleeping better and not waking up during the night. I could walk down a street paved with bricks and not feel nauseous. I felt relaxed and happy.

We'd already traveled through Sicily, Naples, and Rome, and had arrived in Venice for the second half of our trip, an exploration of Northern Italy. We'd be in Venice for a few days before heading to

Verona, the home of Romeo and Juliet. It was silly, but even after everything we'd already seen—Mount Etna in Sicily, Pompeii outside Naples, St. Peter's Basilica in Rome—I was practically beside myself with excitement to see Juliet's balcony. The fact that the most famous setting from Shakespeare's play was a real site that I could visit practically blew my mind.

Not that I wasn't thrilled to be in Venice—Venice!—with its canals and gondolas, its bridges and food, its incredible architecture, and all the art it had inspired. There weren't even any cars on the collection of islands that made up the city! No wonder I felt like I was a world away. It seemed as though I'd been transported one hundred and fifty years into the past. Yeah, the place smelled a little, and some of the buildings were a little less well maintained than they could have been, but I didn't care because it was Venice!

Matt had somehow arranged for us to arrive in the city by sea. We took a train from Rome almost to Venice then got on a boat that went out into the Adriatic Sea before turning back toward the city. It seemed like an odd path at the time but only until the city came into view. Then I understood why Matt had insisted we do it that way. I almost cried when the buildings of Venice appeared. I figured it still counted as almost if the tears weren't actually rolling down my face. My eye makeup got a little smeared, but I avoided black streaks down my cheeks.

There aren't words to describe that moment when you first see a centuries-old city basically appear on the water. It looks like it's floating there, which I suppose it is, in a manner of speaking, but you can't even see the land under it as you approach. It looks like something out of a dream or a movie. A mirage maybe. A Fata Morgana.

I'd been exhausted by the time we got on the boat and wanted to sit on one of the moderately comfortable chairs in the enclosed area of the ferry and maybe doze off a little. I wanted to see Venice as we arrived. I'd heard it was beautiful, but I couldn't imagine it would be that different looking at it through the window. Matt dragged me out to the railing at the bow though, arguing that he hadn't paid for the boat ride just to have me ignore the experience.

"What? Are you trying to *Titanic* me?"

His eyebrows pulled together as he looked at me in confusion.

"You know, Leonardo DiCaprio and Kate Winslet? 'I'm the King of the World'?" I spread my arms out and leaned into him.

He laughed. "Well, that wasn't specifically my plan, but as long as we're out here..." He trailed his voice off and shrugged with a big grin on his face.

I rolled my eyes and turned to look out over the bow. A couple minutes later, when the buildings seemed to materialize over the horizon with the sun setting behind them, no less, I gasped. My hand flew to my mouth, and those tears that didn't actually roll down my cheeks sprang to my eyes. I thought of my mother and my grandparents and how much it would have meant to them to be there, seeing what I was seeing. After they left, my grandparents had never made it back to Italy, and my mother had never managed to visit at all. We'd always talked about taking a mother-daughter trip to see the old country, but we never realized we had as little time as we did. I wished they were there with me, and I supposed that, in some ways, they were.

As Matt slid his arms around my waist, actually *Titanic*-ing me, I realized how lucky I was to be there with a man like him, a man who was smart and funny and successful, a man who valued family and tradition and our heritage as much as I did, a man who would never in a million years hurt and cheat on me like my ex-fiancé, a man who I was hopelessly, head-over-heels in love with.

If swooning hadn't gone out of fashion in the nineteenth century, I would have done it then and there. On the other hand, I was approaching a city that still looked like it was straight out of the nineteenth century, so maybe it wouldn't be unfashionable after all.

After we arrived at the dock, we'd loaded our luggage onto an actual gondola that had taken us to our hotel. The place was incredible. All the hotels we'd stayed in so far had been, but this one was even more amazing than the others. It was old, of course, but its Venetian Gothic architecture was still stunning. The interior was decorated in the gilded, ornate Rococo style that practically had visions of the nineteenth century art salons dancing in my head. The stories I'd heard in my college art history classes about the salons of Venice came back to me in a flurry, and if I squinted, I could almost see John Singer Sargent and James Whistler walking with Claude Monet down the hallway.

We'd been in Venice for eighteen or so hours when we arrived in the Piazza San Marco for lunch. I kept looking around with a giddy expression on my face, not quite believing I was there. The plaza was full of people, but it wasn't what I would call New York City crowded. What was also different from New York was how original everything was—or at least looked. I knew it had all been restored or remodeled more than once over the years, but it wasn't all glass and steel the way modern buildings were.

"You doing all right there?" Matt asked.

"Hmm?"

"I asked if you're doing all right. You're looking around like you're in a daze."

I giggled. "I guess I kind of am. I just can't believe we're here."

Matt grinned as he leaned back in his chair. "After all the places we've been, you're still amazed we're here?"

"After all the places we've been, you're still amazed that I'm amazed?"

"I wouldn't say I'm *amazed*. I'm just glad you're still getting excited about everything. I was afraid that five cities in two weeks was too much, and we'd be too exhausted by now to really appreciate the sights."

"I don't think I'll ever be too exhausted to appreciate sights like this." I gazed around the plaza again. Our café table was on one side of the long arcade that made up two sides of the square. My eyes were drawn to my left over and over again to stare at the ornate church at the east end of the square.

Calling it a church, of course, is an understatement. St. Mark's Basilica is massive and beautiful and historic. It has incredible Byzantine architecture with gilt details that shine in the sun. I wanted to stand up and walk down to it immediately to go inside. I'd studied the pictures online and knew that the interior was every bit as gorgeous as the exterior, if not maybe a little more. I had to restrain myself until the tour Monica's grandson Stefano and his almost-fiancée had arranged for us the next day.

I was beyond excited that they were taking the next two days to show us Venice. Everything you'd ever want to see, they'd arranged to show us. Adriana had even talked a friend of hers who worked for St. Mark's into giving us a private behind-the-scenes tour after the last of the morning celebrations of mass. I had a feeling I'd almost cry again. I thought again about my grandparents and how they'd feel to know that their little Francesca had gotten to go to mass at both St. Peter's at the Vatican and St. Mark's in Venice. I was glad I'd packed waterproof mascara.

Out of the corner of my awe-struck eye, I saw Matt look at his watch.

"We're going to be late if we don't get going"

I glanced down at the tiramisu crumbs on my plate. The dessert had been so delicious I wanted to lick them up. That probably wouldn't look very sophisticated though, so I took a sip of my cappuccino instead.

"Franny?"

"I'm just savoring the rest of my coffee. It's heavenly."

Matt looked down at his empty cup. "It's not that good."

"Don't let them hear you say that."

"What? Yours is better."

I smiled at him. "Liar."

"No, really. This?" He lifted up his cup and tipped it toward me. "This, I could take or leave. Yours? Yours is delicious."

I made a show of peering into his cup. "That didn't seem to stop you from drinking the whole thing."

"I'm not going to pass up a good cup of coffee."

"But you just said—" I stopped and rolled my eyes. There was no use in pointing out to him that he had literally just said that it wasn't that good and that he could take it or leave it.

Matt grinned at me. "Have you tried my coffee?"

I cringed. "Yes. Unfortunately."

"If I drink that, I think you know how low my standards are."

"So I guess maybe my coffee isn't that great after all."

"Nope, yours is perfect. Just because I've been known to eat burnt toast doesn't mean I don't know a good steak when I see it." He stopped for a second. "Well, taste it. I don't actually know if a steak is good by sight."

I giggled and leaned back in my chair. I took another sip of my cappuccino.

"We really do have to go, Franny."

"I know, I just—" I gazed around the square again, taking it all in.

"We'll be back tomorrow. We'll be back tonight. We have reservations for dinner at Caffé Florian, remember?"

I looked across the piazza at the historic café and felt a little flutter of excitement in my stomach. The restaurant had been there since 1720, before the United States was a country, before Italy as it exists today was even a country! Back when Caffé Florian opened, Venice was its own country. I didn't think there even were any restaurants in the U.S. that were that old, and if there were, I'd certainly never eaten in one.

"I know." I sighed but didn't get up.

"Franny."

I glanced into my cup. "Two more sips."

He looked at his watch again. "Get sipping."

I finished off my coffee while Matt took care of the bill. For the duration of the trip, I'd given up on fighting him to pay for anything. "I invited you; I'm paying," he'd said every time I'd tried.

None of my objections about having plenty of money or wanting to pay for something as an expression of gratitude did anything to convince him otherwise. At least he let me pay for the shopping I did. Monica, of course, paid for the shopping I'd done from the list that she had, in fact, ended up providing for me.

"You ready?" he asked when I finally put my cup down.

"I think the more appropriate question is are you ready?" I replied as I stood up. I smoothed the skirt of the simple black-and-white shift dress Rhonda had convinced me to buy. I really was grateful she'd talked me into it. It had a classic silhouette but enough style that it felt modern. And I'd seen enough women on the street wearing similar styles that I didn't feel it marked me as a tourist. In fact, I'd even seen an Italian woman or two look me up and down with approval. I'd seen more than one or two Italian men do that also, but I didn't think that particularly spoke to the fashionable-ness of my dress. I didn't think Matt blended in with the locals quite as well, but enough people had tried to speak Italian to us that

I knew he didn't stick out like a sore thumb. Since arriving in Italy, we'd both realized how embarrassingly bad our Italian was. I had declared more than once that we were taking a class when we got home. Matt nodded when I said it, but I didn't know whether he actually agreed with me.

"No, I still think the right question is whether you're ready. If knives go flying, you're going to be the one standing next to me," Matt said.

"Yes, but your fingers will be closer to it."

"Hmm," he mumbled thoughtfully. I wasn't sure whether he was seriously considering my point or just being silly. He held out his arm to me, and I took it.

The event we needed to get to was an Italian cooking class Monica's grandson Stefano had signed us up for. We were going to make a full traditional meal from the *aperitivo* (appetizer) to the *primo* (first course, usually pasta) and *secondo* (second course, usually meat or fish) all the way through the *dolce* (dessert) and the drinks courses that followed it. Stefano wasn't sure, but he said he thought we were going to make *polenta e schie*, or polenta with shrimp, and a dessert of *pandoro*, a sweet yeast bread. I was excited because Matt would finally learn to make something other than spaghetti Bolognese. I was also excited because I was hoping to pick up a new dessert I could serve at the café.

"*Andiamo cara*," Matt said as we headed into the middle of the plaza, showing off that he knew how to say, "Let's go, darling," in Italian.

We'd reached the middle of the square when he stopped and swung me around to face him. He held on to both of my hands. I tried not to stare at the basilica behind him. He was handsome, but St. Mark's was stunning.

"*Francesca, cara*," he said with a decent enough accent that he actually sounded like he knew more than ten words in Italian.

"*Sì, Matteo?*" I replied, playing along.

"*Sei bellissima, Francesca.*"

I blushed. It wasn't that he didn't tell me I was beautiful all the time, but something about the place and the look in his eyes made it feel extra special. "*Grazie, Matteo.*"

He stared at me for what felt like a long time then shuffled his feet like he was getting ready to start walking again. I started to turn around to leave. "*Francesca?*"

I turned back to look at him. "Sì, *Matteo*?"

"*Francesca—*"

I waited until I realized he wasn't going to say anything else until I did. "Sì?"

"*Ti amo.*"

The tears started down my cheeks before I even realized they'd come to my eyes. I forgot every Italian word I had ever known. I could only raise my voice to a whisper. "I love you too, Matty."

Recipe 1: Latte without an Espresso Machine

Ingredients:

• Espresso or strongly brewed coffee from an Aeropress

• Milk

Make espresso with a Nespresso machine, or use strongly brewed coffee from an Aeropress, undiluted.

Pour milk into a mason jar or any jar with a lid. Fill no more than half the jar. Screw the lid on tight. Shake jar hard for 30 to 60 seconds, until milk is frothy and doubled in volume.

Take lid off jar and microwave uncovered for 30 seconds. The foam will rise to the top of the milk. Heat from the microwave will help stabilize it.

Pour 1/3 cup of espresso into a wide cup. Using a spoon to hold back the foam, pour warm milk on top of the espresso. Spoon as much foam as you like on top of the espresso.

Recipe 2: Ladyfingers

Ingredients:

- 4 eggs
- 2/3 cups + 2 tbsp white sugar
- 1 cup all-purpose flour
- 1/2 tsp baking powder

Preheat oven to 400F. Line 2 baking sheets with parchment. Fit a large pastry bag with a plain ½-inch round tube, or a Ziploc bag with the end cut off.

Beat egg WHITES in a bowl on high until soft peaks form. Add 2 tablespoons of sugar and continue beating until it's stiff and glossy.

In a separate bowl, beat egg yolks and 2/3 cups of sugar. Whip until thick and pale in color.

In a small bowl, whisk flour and baking powder together. Fold half the egg white mixture into the egg yolk mixture. Fold in flour then add rest of egg whites. Transfer mixture to pastry bag.

Pipe stripes, or whatever shape you prefer, onto the sheet. Bake for 8 minutes.

About the Author

Harper Lin is the USA TODAY bestselling author of *The Patisserie Mysteries*, *The Emma Wild Holiday Mysteries*, *The Wonder Cats Mysteries*, and *The Cape Bay Cafe Mysteries*.

When she's not reading or writing mysteries, she loves going to yoga classes, hiking, and hanging out with her family and friends.

www.HarperLin.com

Printed in Great Britain
by Amazon